MW01146164

CRIES OF THE WORLD

THE WORLD BURNS - BOOK 6

BOYD CRAVEN

Copyright © 2015 Boyd Craven III

Cries of the World, The World Burns Book 6
By Boyd Craven

Many thanks to friends and family for keeping me writing! Special thanks to Jenn, who's helped me with my covers from day one and keeps me accountable!!!!!

All rights reserved.

TABLE OF CONTENTS

CHAPTER 1

THE HOMESTEAD, KENTUCKY

Blake and Duncan had taken the Homestead kids into the woods on a foraging trip. It was the end of the mulberry season and they wanted to gather some, if the birds hadn't already stripped the trees bare, and they also planned to get a good look at the nut trees. Fall was coming, and the more they could gather and store, the better they would eat in the winter time. They were both taking the opportunity to get some exercise and educate the kids, who were restless and needed to burn off some energy. Chris was one of them in particular who had been wound up tighter than a kite.

"So you can tell by the leaves and the bark?" One of the older girls, about twelve years of age, was asking.

"Yes, and later on in the year you'll see the nut clusters. If you're out here sitting under a tree and a green ball like this hits you on the head," Blake showed them an aromatic green globe, "then there's a good chance that you're sitting under a walnut tree like this one," he said, rubbing his hands on the bark.

The kids crowded around and Chris asked, "Why would a nut fall and hit you on the head?"

"It's the squirrels' way of getting even," Duncan told them with a straight face.

The exercise had benefits for the men, as well. Blake was nearly healed and Duncan was taking every opportunity, when he wasn't working with the Squad or the folks coming in on basic survival, to try to lose the needed weight. His heart had been bugging him a lot less since Martha had gotten him on his blood pressure medicine, and they had found a pharmacy that wasn't entirely looted on the outskirts of Greenville.

Of course, all the pain pills had been taken, but there was a treasure trove of antibiotics and basic everyday medicines like blood pressure meds that had been overlooked by the looters. All that was fine, but without a way to manufacture more, Duncan knew if he wanted to live a long and happy life and see his grandbaby born, he had to shape up. So walking the hills and the countryside was working for all of them.

"We used to have those by our house. They break open and stain everything," Jeramiah, another kid from the rescued folks, piped up.

"Yeah, they make a big mess. You can hull them a few different ways, but I generally wait till the hulls are almost falling off... But... did you know that you can make dyes out of it?"

"No," they all chorused and Duncan stopped and turned to look at Blake.

"No really, get half a bucket of those hulls, pour two pots of boiling water in and let it sit for a bit. Strain it out and boil it down some. Then, those snare lines I helped you kids make," Blake said, pulling his out of a pocket and showing them, "Then you soak these wires in that, and it takes the shine off them."

"I thought you said most animals don't care about the shine?" Chris asked.

"That's because the animals around our house here have never seen a trap. Later on this year, how many of them do you think are going to get shy of anything shiny?"

Blake let that sink in and Chris was smiling, as he was getting it. Being the son of Blake, he definitely got a little more schooling on this stuff than the others did, but every single one of the kids in the group was a lightning fast learner, from the school of survival they'd all had to attend. It was a rough world, and Blake's group was the only island of peace and prosperity in the area that they knew of.

"So we're going to start staining the snares this year?" Jeremiah asked.

BOYD CRAVEN

"Yes, this fall. That's why I'm showing you all which trees are which. Part of your job this fall is to come out here with a grownup or two and collect all of these nuts. If we have a really cold winter and the animals don't do well, we can eat them. Or..." Duncan paused to drop a wink at Blake, "We can use them to fatten up some hogs and have real bacon."

That announcement brought cheers and whistles from the kids. The home butchered bacon from the wild hogs was good, but it didn't taste the same as the store bought bacon full of chemicals. Weird that something that was worse for you could seem to taste better, but it was something the kids had been talking about nonstop. Not that they complained more than three or four times an hour. Each. About everything, but that was their nature, and the men went along with it as best as they could.

The adults took it in stride and, now that they had a rough sort of schooling set up, the kids found themselves getting frustrated - and with a lot more free time now that the video games, television and all their electronic tethers had been cut. The grownups came up with a plan for them to contribute, and have fun with it. They were also learning how to be self-reliant, and that was something that really mattered to Blake and the family.

"Hey, what kind of tree nut is that?" One of the kids asked, pointing to another tree.

"See how the bark on this one's different? So look at the leaves—" Blake was cut off by his radio.

CRIES OF THE WORLD

"Blake, Sgt. Smith, this is Patty, Sandra's on the horn from the roadside. There's a convoy trying to come up the road. They've stopped it, but she wants you to meet Sgt. Smith and his team and have things set up in case they try to push through. Do you copy? Over."

"Copy that," Blake said.

"Copy, will meet by lane, over," Smith said.

"You want me to come with you?" Duncan asked as Blake put the snare in his pocket and patted himself down, making sure everything was in its place.

"Yeah, let's get the kids to cover, we don't know what kind of convoy they are talking about, and Sandra probably is communicating with base over the scrambled frequencies." Blake said.

"Yeah, I figured that's why she had Patty relay the message to us. That way whoever's out there only hears one part of the conversation," Duncan finished the thought off.

"We can only hope."

§ § §

They double timed it back, enough to make Duncan breathe hard, but he'd been getting better day by day with exercise, good diet and determination… and Lisa hounding him… Arriving at the Homestead house and barn, they were met with half a dozen of the residents who were ready to take the kids into the barn's shelter. They also had some equipment ready for Blake and Duncan.

They had gone over the drill verbally a few times, but never in real life. Fortunately, it worked out flawlessly. They had load bearing vests ready for the men and Duncan's customized M4. He could reach out and crush someone with it. Blake took an AR variant, a semi-automatic that they had looted off one of the many groups of marauders they'd run across that summer. If he wasn't going to be needing his squirrel rifle, he still had his pistol... and this AR-15.

He'd grown somewhat attached to it, appreciating its simple nature once you learned how everything worked and, though it would never replace his deer gun, it was fun to shoot, had little recoil and would definitely work for what it was needed for. The chest rig already had three extra mags fully loaded, so he shrugged out of his .22 and accepted the vest and ran by the house, leaving Duncan to make his way to Sgt. Smith.

"David, Patty, anything you can tell me? Is Sandra still talking on the scrambled frequencies?"

"Yeah, it's some guys who look like soldier of fortune mixed with National Guardsman and Mall Ninjas... with a stuffed suit." Patty answered.

"Stuffed suit?"

"Fat white dude, cowboy hat, blue suit," David answered.

"Got it, anything else?" Blake asked them.

"Claims he's the Governor." Patty answered.

CRIES OF THE WORLD

§ § §

Duncan met with Sgt. Smith and they set up one artillery team, pointing more or less towards the entrance to Holloway Lane. Duncan had already left to go scout out and be a forward observer when Blake caught up to them. One of the men gave Blake a quad and he rode the rest of the way down the hill, loud and proud. The muffled two stroke was the noisiest thing once the artillery had been towed into position.

"Blake?" Sandra's voice asked over the open channel.

Blake slowed so he could use his left hand. He let off the gas before answering, "Yeah, you ok?"

"Squad's fine. Got some folks out here to talk to you. Is that you riding the bike down?"

"Naw, I'm on the quad. Do I need to bring anything for the visitors?" he asked, letting the hill and momentum keep him moving.

"Nope, but these gentlemen want to talk to you. They're starting to get a little impatient," Sandra said.

Something was tickling Blake's senses and he asked, "Any of our friends out there with you?"

"Naw, Corinne and I were walking and these nice folks stopped. Would you hurry up? My legs are sore and I don't want to have to walk home," she answered.

Blake knew she had gone out there with the full squad, and there should have been one squad of

Sgt. Smith's out there under her orders. If she was only claiming that Corrinne was there with her, they must have seen something and got the others out of sight and into ambush positions. They were actively looking for community members to join their homestead or opportunities to help those in need, so maybe it really was the Governor?

Blake put the throttle down and in a couple more minutes he killed the switch and let the quad coast to a stop fifty yards behind where he could see the two ladies standing at the entrance to the lane. He parked behind a large tree, but not so close he'd have to back up to get away. A quick turn and he could be back up the hill or in the brush in moments. And maybe die trying if it came to that, but dying wasn't really on his agenda for the day.

Blake made sure his AR was ready, and hit the transmit button twice on his hand held before walking up. Sandra had her rifle over her back, and Corrinne was standing nervously with her rifle in her hands, pointed at the ground. Blake noticed the ladies' body language first and foremost. Tense, nervous. He knew Sandra could out fight and out shoot almost anybody in any situation, so she must also feel a hint of uncertainty. As he strode up and saw the three truck convoy, he could understand why.

The first vehicle was a military style Hummer, bristling with antennae and looking like an alien bug on steroids. The next was a troop carrier with a canvas side. Half the truck had supplies and the other half was a dozen men jumping off to form a skirmish line. The final truck looked like a semi out of a mad max movie, its paint and bodywork scarred with bullet holes, nicks and scratches. It had an unremarkable trailer, a refer unit Blake thought. They'd parked a hundred yards beyond the girls, in a defensive arrangement.

Standing in front of Sandra was a human pig in a suit. His made Duncan look like a fashion model, and rivulets of sweat stained his collar. Instead of a white suit like Boss Hog wore, he sported a dark navy blue suit.

"Sir, what can I do for ya?" Blake asked, making his voice sound as country as possible.

The man looked him over, his rifle loosely held in his right hand, radio in left. The men looked between the three of them, Sandra rubbing her stomach, trying to emphasize her pregnancy. Blake was confused as to how two seemingly lightly armed women had stopped a convoy of... Mall ninjas? He snickered to himself, remembering the term from the conversation in the house. The soldiers were an odd mixture of uniforms and battle vests. Their armaments were also an odd mix of Russian and American hardware.

"We're here to talk to survivors, take stock of how folks are doing and work with farmers to get the food networks running again," the pig said.

"That sounds like a good plan, but why the soldier boys?" Blake asked, losing his folksy tone immediately as he realized the man seemed rather sharp.

"Look at your lane here," the man motioned with his hands, showing dark splotches of sweat under his arms, "Your homestead is obviously doing well. Well enough that you can have two fine ladies manning the entrance with illegal weapons. Weapons we're going to have to confiscate by executive order—"

"What's it to you? You're not with the US Government or Military," Blake said, taking a guess at what had put the girls on edge.

The lack of formality, the lack of common equipment, and the battered trucks were what was bothering him, though two of them had obviously been military vehicles at some point.

"I'm the interim Governor of the State of Kentucky. Since Louisville fell, we've been rebuilding in the Greenville area. We've had equipment knocking down burnt out buildings, digging graves, working on getting the utilities back..."

Blake let him zone on and looked to his wife. Her lips were smiling, but her eyes were wary. She gave him a shake of the head and nodded to the left where the Governor's men were edging towards cover.

"Whoa, wait a minute guys, you aren't acting all neighborly. This is my property you are fixing to take cover near there," he pointed to the mall ninja on the end of the lineup.

"What it boils down to Mr. Jackson, is we've

been monitoring the open radio and confirmed by DF'ing your signals that you guys are doing all right. I'm here to introduce myself and to take inventory of what you all have in an effort to hurry up the rebuilding process," the governor said.

"What's your name, interim Governor?" Corinne asked suddenly.

The question from another direction threw off the tirade he was building up to, but the Governor turned to her and told her, "John Davis," then he turned his gaze back to Blake but, before he could start talking again, Blake snickered.

"Boss Hogg," he whispered loudly to Sandra, who snorted.

"Oh, my God, I thought I was..." Corrinne cracked up and Blake lost it, letting the belly laughs come out.

"Excuse me, I'm talking to you," John Davis said indignantly.

"Ok, ok," Blake said, wiping his eyes and pulling his rifle off his back again, making the men twitch, but they relaxed after a moment as he kept it aimed low.

"Now, I'm here to go up there and take inventory, so if you'd move your ladies out of the way, my head of security here won't be forced to..."

"Excuse me?" Sandra asked?

"I said move out of our way. We're going to inventory food and provisions for redistribution. It's hot out, and I'm sweating like a pig," which elicited snickers from Corrin and Blake, but Sandra kept her eyes trained on the Governor, "So if you'd tell your head of security we're here - and that you're hopelessly outnumbered…"

"Daddy?" Sandra said into her handset.

"Yes, sugar?" Duncan replied, and his voice coming out of the speakers startled Boss Hogg into stopping the steps he had been taking towards them.

"The Hummer."

"What about the—" Boss Hogg started to ask.

A deep thunk and whistling sound was heard. Even Blake, who was a new guy around towed artillery, knew what that sound was, and the girls almost tackled him. It went to proving how unprofessional the Governor's men were; most didn't recognize the sound until the Hummer was hit by a massive artillery round, setting off secondary explosions as the fuel cans strapped to it went off. Most of the men jumped to the ground or fell as the pressure wave and heat hit them. They were immediately disarmed by the three dozen men, women and young adults that had ghosted out of the woods. The takedown went as they had rehearsed over a hundred times, and it went flawlessly.

"Excuse me, I'm the Governor of Kentucky, you can't…" John Davis said as he was thoroughly frisked.

"Daddy, you have the transport targeted?" Sandra asked into the handset.

"Just give me the word – or I can drop one on

CRIES OF THE WORLD

Jefferson Davis if you'd like," Duncan said with a chuckle.

"Jefferson Davis? John! I'm John Davis!" The outraged governor screamed as the guns were put into a pile, and magazines removed from both men and arms. Then the chambers were emptied.

"Yeah, yeah. I figured that, but you do look like Jefferson Davis Hogg, Boss Hogg." Corinne said, holding her own gun to bear.

Sandra frowned and watched Blake work himself to his feet slowly. He was mostly healed, but sore. He wasn't moving fast enough, so she'd done what she could and tackled him to the ground, using her body as a shield. It was a risky move, but her father had undoubtedly set the first target on the one that held the communications or senior officers. It's what she would have done, and Sgt. Smith's men had performed flawlessly with the hasty plan they had apparently put together.

Blake got up slowly, brushing dirt and gravel off his skin, watching everything happen like he was stuck in slow motion. The concussion of the blast had his ears ringing and the look of sheer shock and horror hadn't left Boss Hogg's face yet. Blake walked over and sat down on the hood of a car they'd pushed onto the side of the road earlier in the summer and let his wife's crew work.

"Didn't hurt the baby, did ya?" Blake asked his wife, concern in his voice.

"Naw, I fell on your head. Pretty soft landing," she smirked.

BOYD CRAVEN

"Cut it out, you two," Corrinne said, smiling big.

"So now that we're being civilized, I'd like you to meet my head of security, Ms. Sandra Jackson here," he said, using her name, since they'd already indicated they'd been following them on the radio.

"John Davis," he said standing up, his red face gone, in its place a pasty white pallor, slightly grey in tone when Blake looked close.

"Governor, we don't take too kindly to people threatening us. I don't know how many people you think we have, but let me tell you... My wife's squad is big enough to overpower you. You're also surrounded by elements of the United States Military and what blew up your fancy hummer was some towed artillery. I think it's a howitzer, but I think it just looks like a big gun. See, I'm just a country boy and a homesteader. I'd like to see some official form or documents if you have any—" Blake was saying but was interrupted by the Governor.

"They were in the—"

"Yeah, sorry about that," Sandra interrupted, "it was to get your attention, or my squad would have had to gun you all down."

"Like I was saying," Blake resumed talking, "my wife is pretty handy with this Army stuff. She was something good, I hear. But most of the rest of us non-military types on the homestead just want to get along and grow our own food. If we can share, we will. As it is, we have an idea about working some of the crops that are going to rot in the fields. There might be excess, but I have no way of knowing

16

who's legit and who's not. None of us do."

"Sir, let me," one of men who looked military from the governor's group asked.

"Sure, sure," he said, and Sandra stepped to the side and started a quiet conversation with him.

Blake turned his attention back at the men that had been disarmed. They had their hands behind their heads in a line on their knees, one leg across the other. They probably thought they were about to be executed, judging by the terrified expressions on their faces and the guns held at eye level to them, but Blake didn't think death was coming for any of them today. He knew his wife wouldn't have ordered the Hummer blown up to make a point if there was somebody inside there. She wasn't like that, and in his heart, neither was he and his.

"I promise you, what I'm saying is true."

"What's in the truck?" Blake asked suddenly, noticing again the refer unit behind the cab of the Semi.

CHAPTER 2

MICHAEL & KING – TALLADEGA FEDERAL PENITENTIARY, ALABAMA

Michael, I really wish you would wait for me," John said, watching the younger man gear up with what was left behind.

"I wish I could, I'm just afraid that if I don't set off after him, I'll never find out where my Mom is," Michael told him.

"Don't you worry," King's deep voice rumbled, sounding like two boulders rubbing against each other, "I'll keep the scrawny kid safe."

"I don't doubt that, and you'll have my thanks for keeping an eye on him," John said, turning and offering his hand to the large black man who'd become one of Michael's closest of friends in the days since liberating the FEMA camp, "but this isn't your fight. Why go?"

"Got nowhere else to be," King said, his voice

18

CRIES OF THE WORLD

so deep he made the narrator from the Lion King's voice sound almost falsetto.

"I can't talk you out of this?" John asked Michael, breaking his grip with King and offering his hand to the young man he'd grown so fond of.

"No, sir. Now that my dad is buried… Lukashenko can't get away. He'll know where the next camp is. We know for a fact that he knew where the women were shipped." Michael told him.

They did indeed. Some of the guards had survived being killed by the prisoners, or they had surrendered. In fact, two of them had locked themselves inside the jail cells that used to house the FEMA inmates. They offered information for their safety. They were still being held in the cells they'd locked themselves into and were proving to be quite a fount of information for the group. Trained interrogators were driving in. Lukashenko would have been the biggest prize and, for reasons John understood, Michael had to go after him.

"You're going to bring him back here, right?" John asked.

Michael hesitated a tick too long.

"Well then, get as much out of him as you can," John said, wanting to say more but knowing it was useless.

Michael had wrestled with enough already, and killing isn't something that's ever easy, just something you learned to put up with. Michael had done more killing in the past few months than most men had ever done in their lifetime, soldiers included. John had seen the kid in action. Most people didn't get that good without a ton of training and experience. Some were born with it, and Michael was one of them. He was passable with a rifle, but it was his father's Colts where he really shone. The kid was deadly with them.

"I will, sir," Michael said, a nervous smile passing over part of his face.

"If it's all the same to you," King rumbled, "I'll kill Lukashenko when we're through with it. I have a score or two to settle with him myself."

"We really need that Intel…" John complained, but King held his hands up for John to stop.

"I was a Major before I got shanghaied and sent downstate here to break big rocks into little rocks. I know what you need. Just give us one of those fancy radios and I'll have him singing." King said, his voice serious but his smile was cold.

"Well damn, how do you figure on doing that?" Michael asked him, surprised at the revelation.

"With this," King held up a stiletto he'd pulled from the small of his back.

"Messy," John said.

"Lukashenko was born an officer; he don't know real pain. I won't have to use it. From what his men were telling me, he's a pompous ass and the men all hated him, except for his inner circle… and they're all dead," King smiled and clapped John on the shoulder before turning and picking up a backpack and rifle from the ground.

"Bye, John," Michael almost whispered.

CRIES OF THE WORLD

"Bye kid." John turned and walked away before his emotions could get the best of him.

§ § §

Breaking camp, John was surprised at the number of people who wanted to stay there. Once the guards were gone or 'handled', about half of the contingent of prisoners elected to stay on and continue the work. The parts were needed and, if the rumors were true, that kind of work would be what it would take to get the country back out of the ashes. The difference was, now they were working for themselves, their families and their country. They would track down the parts needed, and handle the marauders as they found them. Having everyone locked up and concentrated worked for keeping them safe… and prisoners.

Of those who elected to leave, about a quarter were going on a hunt to search out missing relatives or check in on parents, kids and other family members. They tried to encourage them to stick together in large groups to avoid the roving bands of gangs that had formed, but they didn't force them to do so. As it was, John had Linny and Bret to take care of, and he was being asked to handle the planning stages for the next camp. The captured APC would remain for the time being, with a couple of hastily trained operators to protect the camp, its inhabitants and supplies, but eventually it'd be called upon to join in the attack, wherever it may be.

The rest of those leaving were returning to home or to a relative's "farm" in some vague but hard to name town. They 'knew' how to get there. Everyone understood that wasn't the case anymore, but they had seen what it had been like to have their freedoms removed and imprisoned. None of them wanted a repeat of that awful feeling.

John was watching the last of them leave when he felt a gentle tugging on his hand. Small hands, warm. He turned and smiled as he saw Linny and Bret standing there, Caitlin still holding Linny's hand and Bret sneaking glances at the former Miss Maryland. John could understand the kid's distraction, but he knew it was also that Caitlin and Tex had taken in the kids for a day or two. That was another revelation; apparently Tex and Caitlin's banter had been the beginnings of a relationship that nobody could have believed possible.

They'd taken in the kids while John and Michael had been busy burying their dead so they could see if they wanted kids of their own someday. Judging by the smile on Caitlin's face, the little monsters hadn't scared them off child rearing yet. Those two were just good ones.

"Hey guys, are you ready to go camping again?" John asked them.

"Where are we going?" Linny asked.

"With some Army men," Caitlin answered.

"As long as we don't have to eat stinky fish every day!" Bret piped up causing John to chuckle.

CRIES OF THE WORLD

"Stinky fish?" Tex asked, ghosting out of nowhere to put a lanky arm around her shoulders and hug her close to his body.

"Long story," John said, getting himself under control.

"Oh, well then, maybe when we hit camp. Sounds like we have more units coming out of the woodwork and we need to figure out how to set up a central command of sorts. Too many people checking in and no chiefs around here to tell the Indians what to do." Tex told them.

"We'll deal with chain of command when it's time. Let's get everyone together… Here…" John pointed to a map, "where the old fort used to be in the National Forest. There's enough grounds there for all of us."

"Why not just stay here?" Caitlin asked.

John had struggled with that himself, "Because the people who are staying here are building themselves a new life. Having us around would be a constant reminder that they gave up without a fight. That they were rounded up like cattle, and I really hate to admit it but… I don't know if I can keep a straight thought in my head in a place like that. It just makes me want to…"

John's hands balled into fists subconsciously and his knuckles popped. The little kids looked, and realized John was angry, but they didn't say anything. Bret was the first one to break the silence.

"Do you want to go to the cells and get Mr. Jenkins out to hit him again?" Bret asked.

That broke the spell, and John's eyes cleared.

"That sounds like it would work buddy, but that isn't the right thing to do. We're better than that."

"What about the ones you guys lined up by the back wall?" Linny asked.

The grownups winced in unison. The guards who had participated in abuse of the women and young ladies were executed. Each woman was given the option of letting their rapists die by firing squad, or they could elect to do it themselves. Most of the women took the offered combat knives and took their lives back, a brutal but effective way of making sure they got closure. None of the kids were supposed to see it, but the way people talked…

"Those were bad guys, they were the ones who hurt the mommies and sisters," Tex said, pulling Caitlin even closer, his other hand snaking across her midsection in an unconscious move.

"Oh, then that's good! Can we ride in the big tank?" Linny asked, the case closed as far as she cared.

"No, sugar," Caitlin said, "it's going to stay right here and keep the bad guys out."

§ § §

"King, why are you coming with me?" Michael asked after an hour's worth of walking.

"Told you back there, I got nowhere else to be – and a score to settle."

Michael thought about that. Maybe it really was

that simple. King was a big guy, and a man of few words. Dangerous, deadly, and – if truth be told – probably one of the guys who could help Michael safely cross the country, apart from John. John and Michael had argued bitterly about leaving but, in the end, John knew that 17 was old enough to have set your heart on revenge and still too young to be damaged by it when it happened.

John had pulled King's prison files out of curiosity, planning to show them to Michael to prove that his trust in the big man was as flawed as his thinking, but as he read through them, he realized how wrong he was. King had been imprisoned after two youths kicked in his front door while he was asleep. He'd been discharged from the Army at that point and settling into civilian life. He'd given chase and caught the first kid, knocking him out with one blow. He caught up with the second kid and was starting to administer a beating to beat the band when the police showed up.

None of them had properly identified themselves and King had been tackled by one of the cops who thought he was the aggressor and home invader. Without breaking a sweat, King broke the man's arm and collar bone before the second cop tased him and put a gun to his head. The trial was speedy. The youth he'd first knocked out got a home invasion charge, the second one came out of a coma a month later, mostly in one piece. He was charged as well. King, on the other hand, had been charged with assault and battery, resisting arrest and a slew of other charges.

Black on black crime, so it wasn't investigated thoroughly and the police department and the district attorney were trying to save face from the cop who got busted up. The dash camera videos had been released but that wasn't enough to sway a jury; they just saw 'big and ugly', beating on someone when the cop bit off more than he could chew. Two months into his prison sentence, the Aryan Nation took a stab at King in the showers. King broke the would-be assassin's neck and was beating another one almost to death when the guards took him down. He was in solitary confinement for months afterwards.

You'd think that'd be it, but then he was charged with the murder of the first man, same as the skinhead who lived. They tacked on more time. The second attempt on his life came a year later and that time King felt he needed to send a message if he was to be left alone. He'd be imprisoned for life, but he'd be alive. They came for him in the laundry, where he was working. He'd gotten in-between a row of machines where they had to come for him single file, and he broke the arms of the first man before breaking his neck, turning his head all the way around.

When he threw the body into the pile of awaiting skinheads they went ballistic. Two more died before the guards had everything locked down and King had earned himself the notoriety needed to ensure nobody tried again, as long as he didn't appear to be 'getting soft. Every now and then he needed to demonstrate how brutal and bad he was, but he never wanted to kill anybody. Circumstances and how people seemed to take offense at his color and size forced him to act just like they expected him to.

When John shared all of that with Michael, the kid just nodded. Then Michael recounted his own problems with Jeff at first and then later on with both Jeff and Les. He wouldn't have believed the story if King hadn't been there smiling like the Cheshire cat in the dark.

"Law of the jungle, baby," King said, his voice startlingly deep to John's ears.

"Respect and power," Michael answered.

"You know, it's a brutal world out here right now, maybe that will keep you alive for a while, but you can't lose your humanity," John told them both.

"You can't lose your humanity if you're dead," was King's last word on it.

All of that was going through Michael's head as they walked. They had been offered one of the running trucks that the FEMA camp had confiscated but they'd declined, planning on picking up something else on the way out of town. They had no idea where, but they wanted to keep the running vehicles for those with kids and wives. They were loaded down for bear, having looted the NATO weapons the guards had pre-positioned in one of the cells in Solitary of all places. King wore a combat vest without a shirt, with an H&K USP in a clamshell and extra magazines.

"Never was good with the rifle, don't know how they kept me in," was what he'd said when they'd offered him one.

Michael had his grandfather's old grease gun and his father's matching Colts with enough cartridges and magazines to make walking a struggle.

"Hey, King, what happens after we settle things with Lukashenko and get my mom back?" Michael asked, curious and a bit afraid of the answer.

"Well kid, how about we figure it out when we get there? Lots of miles between us and Louisiana."

"Louisiana? That's where we're going?" Michael asked.

"Yeah, I heard of a camp down that a way that Lukashenko did trades with. Worst comes to worst, we could always let ourselves get captured. Might save us some walking."

"Yeah right," Michael chuckled, "that worked out well for me last time…"

CHAPTER 3

THE HOMESTEAD, KENTUCKY

The refrigerated truck was filled with a variety of hanging carcasses. Cow, deer and wooden crates of what appeared to be processed chickens, all layered in sheets of plastic.

"Where'd all the food come from?" Blake asked John Davis.

"I told you, we're doing an inventory of the surrounding areas. We're working with people to redistribute food to those in need."

Blake thought about that a moment and was about to answer when he noticed Sandra's little pow-wow with the Governor's head of security was over. He held up a finger to Davis and walked over to her.

"That could have been hairy," Blake admitted.

"Yeah. I talked to Sgt. Silverman over there,"

Sandra pointed to him, "It actually sounds legit to some degree. I guess by having the radio station we caught their attention."

Blake let that sink in before answering, "I'm sorry, I just wanted to help. I didn't realize doing this was jeopardizing everyone's safety."

"I said to some degree," she swatted at his arm playfully, "but they did forcibly take food from some people they called 'hoarders' and more from a big cattle operation about an hour from here."

"How is that legit then?" Blake asked, his voice angry.

Sandra smiled, she knew the anger wasn't directed at her, "Right now, there isn't any real form of government, from what Silverman was saying. Each state's Governor was told to activate the National Guard, Martial Law, blah, blah, blah."

"Blah, blah, blah?" Blake asked, "Are we getting into technical Army terminology here?"

"Yep, it's in the manual," she teased.

"I don't like that they took that food by force," Blake nodded towards the truck, "and if they are the good guys..." his words trailed off and he looked over at Davis.

"I know, trust me Baby, I know. The real question is, now what?" Sandra poked him in the side and grinned when Blake jumped.

"Why are you asking me?" Blake asked, ready to have asked his wife the same question.

"Because, oh fearless leader, this is your family's homestead. Oh, and because you're our fearless

CRIES OF THE WORLD

leader."

"No, no I'm not. I'm just a blogger and country boy," Blake told her.

"Not anymore," Corrinne said, walking up to them.

"What do you think?" Blake asked Corinne, nodding towards Davis.

"Don't try to take anything by force. You…" Corrine took a deep breath, looked away a moment and wiped her eyes, "You and your family got me and a lot of other people out of a very bad situation." Corinne said, referring to the slavers, "They were supposed to be the bad guys. Now the good guys are basically acting the same way? I don't know; if this is as Boss Hogg says it is… I don't know. I just don't know." She turned abruptly and walked towards the tree line.

Blake took a deep breath and went over to John Davis and his head of security. Pulling a folding knife out, he gently took the Sgt.'s arm and cut the zip tie off, and then did the same for Davis.

"Thank you sir," Sgt. Silverman said, rubbing his wrists.

"So," Davis said with a sneer, "Are you ready to let us inventory your supplies and take appropriate actions?"

"No," Blake said softly. "I'm not against doing my part and helping out, Governor. Truthfully, I think we'll have just about enough for our own people up in the hills. We're not sitting on Solomon's mine up there, no matter what you think you heard from the radio."

"Listen, by executive order I have the right to—"

"Act like a thug? A bandit? A Thief? Listen Davis," Blake said, grabbing him by the lapels of his sweat soaked suit jacket, "We've been dealing with thugs, bandits and thieves ever since the power went out, including rogue factions of the government were either buried shallowly or left out for the animals to pick over. Like I said earlier, I don't mind helping if we have extra… But until we get some of the bigger farm machinery working, we have just about enough for us. When we get that going, I'll be in a better position to share." Blake said, his anger rising making him red in the face.

"Oh yeah? Buried them all?" Davis said, knocking Blake's hands away, "So you are admitting to attacking government forces? Look at you and your people," Davis said, motioning with his hands.

"Yeah?" Blake asked, not sure where the question was going.

"Every single one of them is healthy and not a single one looks like they've gone hungry," Davis snarled, spittle coming out of his mouth.

"You don't look like you're starving yourself, Guv."

That almost sent Davis into a rage, but Sgt. Silverman put his arm up to stop the charge.

"Most of my city is dead! People are starving. We're trying to rebuild in a structured manner according to FEMA guidelines—"

Blake interrupted, not able to hold back, "How

CRIES OF THE WORLD

is it you're not starving? Or did you lose a couple hundred pounds in the crash diet? Listen," he paused as Davis tried to surge at him again to be held back by Silverman, "Listen, maybe staying in the cities doesn't make sense anymore. Not until you get the services back up and running. There's nowhere to grow food, nowhere to farm, nowhere to dispose of waste… Your water quality is probably horrible—"

"Those are all problems we're dealing with. There's just too many people and not enough infrastructure to support them. People are dying," Sgt. Silverman answered, hiding a placating hand up in front of Davis.

"I'm not heartless," Blake continued. "I basically have the same issues you do, but I can at least grow or hunt my own food out here. You get me the parts and a couple mechanics and I can probably help everyone out. I've got quite a few farm families here with crops in the fields with no way to harvest or transport. If you can help with that, I can help with the food." Blake said, telling them what he'd been thinking about already.

"Now that sounds reasonable," Silverman said, looking at Davis, who seemed to be calming down.

"You know, you don't have any right to refuse us. I was given authority—"

"Oh, stop," both Silverman and Blake said at the same moment.

Surprisingly, Davis shut up, but shot Silverman a death glare.

"Listen Davis, I don't think you have enough men or manpower or working equipment to take us by force. If you're legitimate, I'm willing to work with you. Isn't that worth more than empty threats and chest thumping?"

Davis glowered.

"Are my men free to go?" Silverman asked.

"I'll have to ask my wife how we handle that part. I'm just a homesteader." Blake admitted, walking away from Davis with Silverman in tow.

"I appreciate you not killing us outright. I've been telling that fool you can't roll up on people like that, not when we have no Intel. He could have gotten us all dead." Silverman's face was hard and mostly expressionless.

A hint of anger showed through his expression, though, no matter how hard he tried to hide it. Blake marveled at the man's self-control. He'd just been humbled, and his professional skills put to a test which he'd failed.

"Do you agree with all of this?" Blake asked, motioning to the transport and reefer truck.

"No, but the orders are legit and legal."

"What about some of your guys, they aren't all military, are they?" Blake asked.

"No, there's scum and merc's mixed in with my men. It's a disgrace. I think half of them are criminals. Honestly, if we weren't so short handed, I'd have them digging latrines back in the city just to keep the stupidity away from me and my men," Silverman said, starting to calm.

CRIES OF THE WORLD

"Why do you stick around with this outfit then? I mean, you took an oath… Don't you and your men feel that operating like this is breaking it?" Blake waited as the pause between replies grew and grew.

"Tell you what, in a week or so I'll see if I can scare up a few mechanics and parts. We'll sit down and have a cold beer. I'll fill you and your men in."

"And women," Sandra said sweetly.

"And women, but I don't think you're going to be drinking, Ma'am." Silverman said, a smile tugging at the edges of his mouth.

"Blake, I can fix just about anything…" Sandra started to ask.

"No babe, you've got too much going on. Besides, the baby—" Blake said before Silverman interrupted.

"Ma'am, I do have to warn you though, by executive order… All military and ex-military have been activated and pressed into service. I do believe that means—"

Blake cut in. "No, she's pregnant and she isn't going anywhere right now."

"I'm in no position to force the issue, I'm just passing the word along. I imagine that as soon as things get more organized…" Silverman broke off and Sandra nodded.

"We'll see. Right now it sounds like we've got NATO running our country. There's been no new legal orders coming out from our government, so until there is… I'll stay right here. I'm sure most of us will actually." Sandra told him, her arm snaking around Blake's waist.

"You got room for a few more?" Silverman asked, chuckling and walking away.

"Do you think he was serious?" Sandra asked.

"I think so," Blake told her.

§ § §

Later that afternoon, the security team met up to debrief and Sandra, Duncan and Sgt. Smith talked about what worked and what didn't. It was a mixture of former military and Sandra's squad with some homesteaders thrown into the mix. Nobody had been hurt, besides the Humvee. Other than having an elevated watch placed on the end of the lane, and a couple of spotters further down the road, it turned into a normal afternoon. A little more excitement than they were used to lately, but a good reminder to always be ready and always be on guard.

It also gave Blake time to get back to the house in time for Rebel Radio. He didn't have a prepared topic for the evening broadcast, but he had a vague idea what he wanted to talk about, compliments of one Boss Hogg, John Davis. Government outreach, rebuilding etc. What had happened that day could have been bloody for either side, though it was mostly going to be the governors' men if they were the ones who had tried to push things!

Someone somewhere had a cassette player and when David keyed up the mic, a kid in California

CRIES OF THE WORLD

played Gorilla Radio. Lisa began dancing a little bit and Duncan laughed. Sandra slid in next to Blake and almost giggled at the sight. Lisa had confessed her love for Rage Against The Machine a while back, but this had been a new angle and a new twist. Maybe they could switch things up as old technology was found that still worked, or they could make new technology when the country started the rebuilding process. If it made the listeners as happy as it did the homesteaders, it was worth the effort.

"Good evening everyone, this here is Blake Jackson, Back Country J from my blogging days. Welcome to another Rebel Radio broadcast. Tonight, I'd like to tell you a story and then ask all of you a question. This is going to be more interactive than you're probably used to, but I'm downright curious what you all think about the situation I have going on.

"See, the interim governor showed up at our property today to take inventory of our supplies in order to redistribute them to those in need. If I thought we'd have a ton extra, I'd probably do it. You all and Lord knows how many survivors we've brought into the Homestead, but until we can get a way of getting more food to mouths, we just can't give up what they were asking. Now, I don't know if they're legit but I have a feeling they were.

"See, they came in with troops and mall ninjas according to my lovely wife," he said pausing to look at her.

Sandra took the microphone and hit the transmit button, "Yes, mall ninjas," and handed it back.

"So that didn't go down well and we had to send them away empty handed. If their stories are legit, it sounds like they are trying to set things back up in the cities. That doesn't make any sense to me right now and, from what I hear, big cities are even worse than the camps. Especially if you had an airport nearby…"

Blake let that trail off a minute. He'd heard the figures from somebody on the broadcast once. 5,000 airplanes in the sky over the United States at any given moment. 9/11 happening in an instant, thousands of times over, and the devastation had been horrific.

"So, if folks like this are legit and want to take your supplies or force you into camps by executive order… I mean… The Constitution and the Bill of Rights have basically been suspended. Now, we have NATO 'Peace Keepers' – and I use those words loosely – helping to enforce things because of scattered resources and personnel that didn't show up," Blake said and broke off.

"You can do this," Sandra whispered to him, rubbing his shoulders.

They had talked about it earlier, and a government that wanted total control, such as John Davis had alluded to, was no government they wanted to work with. That was treason, pure and simple, and every person at the homestead would have to make a decision. They'd mentioned that all troops were being activated, current and former, and to report in. The messages that Sgt. Smith had been getting weren't too far off if the Governor was legit…. But how to vet that?

"So do we want a government that wants to come in, take half of everything we got and send it to the cities and refugee camps for redistribution? I've prayed over this and I kind of think if I get extra and I can afford to give away I will, but is that the right thing to do? I don't know. I'd love to hear from all of you, because I'm sitting pretty remote here and I'm sure you've all had to do come to this decision much sooner than I did. Over." Blake sat back and waited.

There was a long pause, and only the static was on the air. Blake started to sweat, never had there been a silent frequency. Had he pushed things too far? Was his traitorous attitude too much for them? He'd been a loner and a blogger forever. All he wanted to do was to do his own thing, but if he could help someone else out, that would be great. Lately, he'd been doing it over the radio. That didn't make him a DJ or even more of an extrovert, he just looked at it as one more way to help and teach.

"Hey Blake, how many of them walked away?" a male voice asked.

"All of them," Blake replied.

"Mighty generous of ya. I figured you've got the biggest mobile Army in the middle of the country. I don't know why they would poke the bear like that.

BOYD CRAVEN

Hell with them, it's Martial Law right now and even the people in charge aren't always the best for the public. Heck, we saw that with the President - and I have no clue how he got elected to a second term. Over," the man said, and Blake had to smile.

If it didn't turn into a political discussion, they might actually be able share some information.

"Sandra," David said, his headset half pulled away from his ear, "I've got a Lieutenant or Sargent Silverman on the scrambled unit asking for you. He's asking for authentication. You want this?" he asked, showing the portable handset with the combo headphone/mic.

"Yeah, I'll take it," Sandra whispered as Blake's radio came alive with more people weighing in on the subject.

"Wait one," she said into the mic and gave Blake a hug before heading towards the bedroom.

"Ok, that's a good point," Blake told someone, trying to steer the conversation back on topic, "But if there was a way to help, how do you tell the good guys from the bad ones? I mean, I had a rogue guard unit buying and selling humans just months ago. This was part of the government. They claimed they were legit, I'm sure acting within what *they* felt was Martial Law... But, they still did what they did. I don't want to get into a shooting war with the legitimate government, but every single one of them was wanting to shoot first, take what they wanted and... Sorry, I'm getting worked up. I want to hear from you."

CRIES OF THE WORLD

§ § §

Sandra read off a set of numbers and Silverman read a different set back. When Boss Hogg wasn't looking, he'd slipped a piece of paper to her. A code so they would always know if the person on the other end was actually the ones talking to them, or that they weren't under duress. It was pretty simple but effective. Sandra would tell him 10 9 8 7 6 for example, and for however long the number was, you added numerically at a prearranged spot and add them together. 10+1, 9+2, 8+3, 7+4, 6+5, turned into 11, 11, 11, 11, 11 for example. It was supposed to be the ultimate double safety check, and no, they didn't start with 1-10, that would have been too simple.

"You got my attention Silverman, over." Sandra said.

"You guys really thumped Davis's nose bad today. Are you guys truly looking for a fight? Over."

"Not looking for one, but we've dealt with the corruption from the government already. Don't know who is for real or not. The fact you guys had a trailer full of food you took from others… I don't know. You guys are no better than the raiders. Over," Sandra retorted.

"I was just following orders, over."

"So were the Nazis. Over.

There was a long pause.

"You're going to have to start picking a side, sooner or later. Over," Silverman said quietly.

41

"What side is that? Over."

"Whether or not to join or bow to the new government that's being formed or to fight it, be self-contained. Over," Silverman said, but he sounded disgusted at the thought.

"New Government?" Sandra asked, losing the etiquette most used on the radio. It was a pretty obscure channel, one she'd given him as a just in case. She hoped this wasn't the just in case.

"Yeah, there isn't much in the way of command here and the President's final orders are being carried out. With most of the house and senate gone now, it's really hard to say what's going to happen. I heard Blake on the radio and decided I had to choose my own side finally. For me, my men and our families. Over."

Sandra kicked back and sat on the edge of the bed. Laying down, she looked up at the ceiling.

"What side is that?" Sandra asked him, wondering if she was going to get any answers or if he was wasting her time.

"Well, our guys, and not the merc's that Davis brought along, are the real soldiers. A bunch of us don't feel comfortable with our orders and we all plead an oath to the constitution. Now that's getting scrapped and those in charge are talking about a reset. I'm not high enough in the food chain to know much, but I overheard a lot. Listen, I'm probably bugging out sometime soon, AWOL. With our troops and families still loyal to the USA. I just wanted to let you know that in case Davis does something stupid. It's not me and it's not us."

"I will. It sounds like you're expecting some sort of revenge attack by the sound of it? Davis getting his ass handed to him probably has him all up in arms, doesn't it? Over."

"Yeah Sandra, I really think he is. It can't be tomorrow, but he was spitting mad and talking all kinds of shit on the trip back into the city. If he goes through with half of what he's threatening…" Silverman's words drifted off.

When it was clear he'd finished his thought, Sandra keyed the mic. "Ok, will keep in mind. You'd literally have to have more than a battalion strength to even bust in here," she lied, "so I'm not overly worried."

"Remember, this is not me. I'm out. I'm leaving with whoever will go in the next day or two. He'll probably blame that on you guys as well. Listen, I have to run. Over and out," Silverman said.

"Over and out." Sandra replied, staring at the ceiling.

"This day keeps getting better and better," she murmured and went out to the living room as Blake's part of the broadcast just got finished up.

They'd turned the frequency back over to those who listened to talk about the government, conspiracies and things that would really have sounded crazy to Sandra, if she hadn't just gotten off the radio with somebody close to what was actually going on.

"You good?" Sandra asked Blake.

BOYD CRAVEN

"Yeah, we're all set here. Want to go see if Chris is done with school?" Blake asked, stretching.

"You betcha," she poked him in the side and laughed when he squirmed out of the way for a second one, "but we have to talk."

CHAPTER 4

THE HOMESTEAD, KENTUCKY

Sandra filled Blake in, and he took it all in, nodding. It was what he'd been expecting, apparently.

"You do what you have to do," Blake told her, kissing the tip of her nose.

"Well, I was planning on it, but we may have to do more than anti-personnel traps now, and not all of it from the Homestead property," she told him.

"You're the expert on that, I'm just a simple country boy," Blake grinned.

"Dammit, no you're not. You're a survivor, an organizer. There's nothing simple about what you do, except that you prefer the quiet of the woods to the usual mess the rest of us put up with," Sandra said, exasperated.

"I don't know about all of that. You and your

father, the Cayhills… you all are more responsible for how we've turned out than just me."

"Blake, you're ducking the issue. We need to figure out if these guys hit us, do we hit them back?"

"What do you mean?" he asked.

"You take out a Special Forces squad, do they send in armor? You take out the armor, do they send in aerial? There's an escalation about to happen and I don't know how far it'll go. The Governor seems to be acting with Presidential authority, and the troops seem to be listening to it for now. Him coming out here was probably supposed to wow us that the big dog in the state thought it was a good idea to visit with us, but I don't know…"

"You're worried about a civil war?" Blake asked her, pulling her close into his arms.

"Yeah," Sandra said.

"I don't recognize a government that would take food or livestock from people who are already starving. That just doesn't make sense to me. There's food they could grow, wild edibles to forage…"

"I know, but not everyone is you," Sandra said.

"I'm just a simple country boy…."

Sandra turned and kissed him deeply, "No, you're my husband and I love you."

"I love you too," he told her.

"So let me get my dad and Sgt. Smith in on this, but I have a plan," she said grinning.

"You always do. You're like the guy from the A team who always has a plan," Blake said.

"I'm just glad you didn't say I was Mr. T," she

slapped at his arm as they walked back towards the barn to collect the kiddo.

"No, because then I'd be Murdock."

§ § §

"I see two transports, full. Over," Corinne's voice came to Sandra over the scrambled frequency.

"What are they doing? Over."

"Offloading. About twenty in each… Oh shit, they're going to assault us, aren't they?" Corrinne asked.

"Looks like it. Daddy, hit the first transport as soon as it's empty." Sandra said.

Blake was listening in over the radio. The plan was pretty much brilliant, in his opinion. The only way to approach the Homestead through the woods was the same way the Slavers had. There was a small valley that ran between them and, if you didn't know someone was there, they could move pretty much unseen. If you already knew they were coming, you could create a kill box with both sides of high ground manned by Sandra and Sgt. Smith's men and women. They had a few scenarios planned out, but sending twenty to forty armed men made the most sense.

"Go," Sandra said.

Blake heard the deep thunk sound and a whistling sound, and then another and another. The first round was HE and the next rounds were going to be AP rounds. When Sandra and Duncan explained what an AP round was, he shuddered. He never wanted to be under barrage by anything remotely like that. None of it really, if he had his choice, but he didn't know how the governor would react.

"Forces fleeing into forest," Karen, one of the women rescued from the slavers and now a part of Sandra's squad, reported.

"Ok, radio silence until we spring the trap."

Blake waited; the silence was killing him. Chris walked out of the bedroom, but Blake waved him back in. Reluctantly, he went in and closed the door again. Just in case, he didn't want the little man to hear something he shouldn't, but all the kids were with adults or in a shelter until the situation was taken care of. It was something they all knew they were going to have to deal with, so the day before everyone had prepped, and scouted locations had been prepared ten miles in each direction to hopefully prevent the Governors' men from dropping artillery on them.

He knew it was a possibility and there were bigger units than what they'd had at the Homestead, but there weren't enough people to cover every road that could potentially lead to the Homestead. Careful planning and judicious use of educated guesses were used to come up with the plan.

"Closing the lid," one of Sandra's squad said, her voice so low Blake couldn't make it out.

David and Patty just sat there, quietly, listening as well. It was a macabre event, listening to mass

CRIES OF THE WORLD

death about to occur, even if it was at the hands of their own military. The world had become a strange place indeed.

"Springing trap," Sgt. Smith said.

Even without the radio, the gunfire could be heard up at the main house and Blake went and opened the front door of the house and looked out, praying his wife was away from the mess. She'd promised to stay out of the action, but she was a warrior. He knew she wouldn't be able to for long.

The gunfire petered out and Blake heard Sandra's voice from the radio, "Mop Up. Save me one. Over."

Single shots rang out. Mopping up usually involved a shot to the head before they considered somebody dead. By the sound of it, they'd be lucky to have found any, let alone one alive.

"Casualty report? Over," Duncan asked.

"None from our side," Sandra said back, "Other side looks to be total—"

"Sandra, I have one by the second troop transport. Must have hid under the truck when the AP rounds were going off, over."

Blake smiled in relief. Nobody even got dinged or scratched from their side. He turned the volume down on the main unit for a moment and went and got Chris, who was looking at him angrily.

"I don't like to be in here if I'm not in time out or sleeping," Chris told him, his arms folded.

"There was a big fight and I was listening in making sure Mom didn't get hurt," Blake told him.

BOYD CRAVEN

There was indecision in Chris's eyes and Blake pulled him off the bed and held him. He grunted as a muscle threatened to cramp, but it didn't. He was finally healing up the rest of the way.

"Let's go and wait for her to come back," he told the little man.

"Can we wait by the bunnies?" Chris asked, a smile cracking the edges of his face.

Blake thought about it. The rabbit colony pen wasn't close to where he expected Sandra to come back in, but you could see when she did.

"Sure!"

He put Chris down and had to laugh as the young boy went running, carefree, towards the barn's southern edge where the outdoor run had been constructed. It was one of the favored spots for the kids to play around. It had bugged them at first, a couple weeks before, when the older grow out rabbits had been removed and processed, but then there was always a new batch of babies, or kits, to love on.

Blake boosted Chris over the side and then took a big step himself over. Immediately, white rabbits with brown/black markings on their nose, ears and feet hopped over to see what the human slaves had brought in terms of treats. Since Blake came empty handed, he just sat there next to Chris as Sheila, one of the breeding does, hopped over. She nudged Blake's hand and he began petting her. Blake was half distracted looking out over the hill and Chris's shrill laugh jerked his attention back.

CRIES OF THE WORLD

Three of the babies had hopped over and one was on his lap, hind legs holding it up as the front legs reached towards his chin. It was licking Chris's shirt and that had caused the giggles. Used to the loud outburst from kids, the rabbits weren't concerned by Chris's noise.

"We have to build that fodder setup that the new guys were telling us about," Blake said to himself.

"For Door?" Chris asked.

"Fodder. Where we sprout the seeds and let it grow a little bit. I want to try it for wintertime if we can't put up enough hay for the animals," Blake told him.

"Sounds gross," Chris said and then stood, the rabbits falling off his lap as he pointed.

Blake stood as well and, coming out of the woods, was about 1/3 of the group that had gone out. Leading it was Sandra and Duncan.

"Up?" Chris begged.

Blake boosted him up and over in time to see Lisa coming up. Her whole face lit up when she saw Chris, and she held out her hand.

"Grandma, let's go get Mom!"

"Wait for me," Blake told them, standing and stepping out of the run.

Together, the three of them walked down the hill, to see a stern-faced Duncan with an equally stoic Sandra.

"Hey, you guys ok?" I asked.

"They weren't even real soldiers," Sandra said after a minute. "It wasn't war, it was a…" she paused as she saw Chris looking at her expectantly.

"Hey, Momma, what are we going to have for dinner tonight?" He asked.

Blake laughed, which just caused Lisa and Sandra something to give Blake 'the look'. Normally that would have been enough to shake off any joking mood, but the tension had been so thick it was laugh or cry.

"Come on, we'll go figure something out. Probably squirrel turds," Sandra told him with a straight face.

"I thought you said Dad was the only one who was nuts?"

Duncan joined them and they all stood there as Lisa, Chris and Sandra walked up the hill.

"How bad was it?" Blake asked after a moment.

"Shooting fish in a barrel. The artillery scared them so bad after the first round…"

"Where's everyone else?" Blake asked.

"Gathering equipment, supplies and towing the troop transport away with the first one. It's pretty well shot from the AP rounds, but it's drivable. We're using that to tow the remains of the first. About half the folks are cleaning it up back there, hopefully so it doesn't look like we bush whacked them like we did. I doubt there were any real soldiers in that bunch," Duncan said and crossed himself.

"They were probably the same sort of merc's that tried to show up last time." Blake told him.

"Yeah, they looked like they were all dressed from *Soldier Of Fortune Magazine*." Duncan admitted.

"I'm just worried what they're going to try to do next," Blake admitted.

"Me too kid, me too."

§ § §

Two days passed with no issues and no word from Silverman or the Governor. Blake went back to his usual morning routine of taking the kids into the woods. With fall almost upon them, the black walnuts would be ready or almost there. The trick was to beat the squirrels, as the critters would stash and bury every nut they could find. Each kid was given a sack to collect whatever it was they found. They'd all avoided going through the areas where the gun battle had been in for obvious reasons. The sun was out in full force and soon everyone was sweating.

"Why can't we have regular school?" one of the teenaged girls griped.

"Well, this is important too. Maybe as much as math and reading." Blake told her.

"Why though? You guys always have food. There's still a ton of it stored in the barn."

"What do we do when that runs out?" Blake asked.

"We go to the… Ok, ok. So why is this important?" she asked.

"Truth is, what happens if something happens to me, or the other grownups, or you get lost out here on your own? What happens when the food in the barn is gone? Part of what I'm teaching you is to survive and thrive. Gathering nuts is going to help us a ton in the winter time, trust me! Besides, it keeps you out of Duncan's hair... or lack thereof," Blake said with a grin.

"I did hear that," Duncan said from the back of the group.

"Sorry Dad," Blake said, grinning.

"So someday, what we're learning is going to make us like Behr Grylls?" a younger boy asked.

"Who's that?" Blake asked.

"He's Survivor Man, or someone like him," the boy answered sheepishly.

"I think I saw that on YouTube," Blake muttered and they all chuckled.

It took them two hours, but they filled every bag with nuts or berries. The late mulberries were sweet and tart. According to Melissa's father Curt, it could be made into an excellent wine. Since booze, beer and wine had all disappeared fast, they were considering starting to make their own. It would be six months to a year before they found out if it was any good, but they could always use the rest of the berries that weren't juiced for jams, pies and jellies.

The kids ate berries and grazed on the wild strawberries that grew on the hills in open places. It was peaceful and, as they walked, Blake pointed out the game trails and explained trapping techniques. They were able to collect a couple of rabbits from the snares they'd already put out and those would go towards dinner too, but they'd been hoping for something else. They had enough rabbit.

"I want to try for a few more hogs soon," Blake told Duncan as they broke the woods and the kids ran towards the barn.

"Fire up that smoker of yours again?" Duncan asked.

"I do love some bacon. Honestly though, we need to get some more salt soon. We're running low and when we run out of processed foods…"

"Oh, we'll find some," Duncan said, "Loads of houses down here used a water softener. Rock salt is cheaper than water softener salt, so we can probably find it by the ton somewhere. Build you that salt box you've been talking about."

"Yeah, if we only had enough salt." Blake groused.

"Blake, Dad, can you drop the kids off and meet me down by the end of the trail? The guy we captured is ready to talk in exchange for us cutting him loose." Sandra's voice said.

"Sure, give us a little bit," Duncan said into his handset.

"Never ends, does it?" Blake asked his father in law.

"No, it never does. Let's go."

CHAPTER 5

MICHAEL & KING

Two days on the road had left Michael sore and wishing they'd taken one of the trucks. Sleeping on the ground was something that he hadn't missed when he had gotten imprisoned in the FEMA camp. If anything, that was the only comfort they'd had there. Instead, they had some thin foam sleeping pads rolled up with their packs that seemed to weigh even more as the day wore on.

"Good spot for water," King pointed to a bridge crossing the road.

Beneath it, a stream ran. Michael didn't say much, he was already exhausted. They dropped their packs and pulled out their canteens and water bottles. King had insisted on bringing some Katadyn life straws, but they didn't want to put

CRIES OF THE WORLD

non-potable water in their containers unless they had to. They knew the bleach trick, and even had some purification tablets that John had given them but, for the time being, they were going to use the hand pump filter.

"Your turn," Michael said, smiling for once.

"Naw, it isn't. No worries, I got you little man," King said smiling.

King ran the hand pump, one tube running into the fast moving stream, away from the sediment, and the other ready to pour out the filtered water. It wasn't a perfect solution, but pumping nonstop was another thing to make one sore if you weren't used to it. Even after a whole summer living in the rough, Michael wasn't used to it, but it was better than drinking the chemical water.

King dropped the filter and pulled his handgun as a canoe came into sight under the bridge. Silent, it had floated under without making a sound and an old man paddled with a shotgun across his lap.

"Morning boys," the old man said.

"Hey," Michael said, grabbing the filter unit out of the water.

"Morning," King said.

"Fishing's pretty good today huh?" the old man said, aiming the boat towards the shoreline where they were standing.

"Be ready," King whispered, which made Michael worried.

King never whispered. He was loud, intimidating and raw power. The overly cautious part of him had put Michael on edge. He couldn't go for his rifle without alerting the old man, but his hand wasn't too far from his .45. He kept his gun hand free and walked to the edge where the canoe was grounding itself against the rocky shoreline. That earned him a frown from King, but Michael was worried about being bunched up too tight with that shotgun the old man had. This way if things went south he'd have to pick which way to fire first and that would definitely result in bad things happening.

"Here, kid, hold this for me, will you?" the old man said, handing the shotgun towards Michael, butt end first.

King tensed and then relaxed as Michael took the gun. Immediately, he broke open the old double barrel and held it over his shoulder, letting his free hand steady the canoe as the man stepped out.

"I'm Carl, just fishing today. Went upstream and caught me a couple catfish and some largemouth. You guys camping through here?"

"No sir," Michael said, "We're traveling and stopped for some water."

Michael was still wary, but the man nodded and held out his hands for the shotgun. Michael handed it back, trying not to look nervous and reluctant.

"Best to boil the water here. People get sick from untreated water nowadays." Carl told them.

"Yes sir," Michael said, watching King watch them.

"This your camp?" King broke his silence.

"Sort of. I got a place a little further down but

CRIES OF THE WORLD

I can't pull my canoe out of the river anymore. So when I get some fish like I do today, I land it and then carry things a little at a time before floating down and tying off. Makes me work harder, but life in the boondocks has always been like that," Carl told them.

"You know about the power being out?" Michael blurted out.

Carl laughed and nodded. "I'm old and a bit of a hillbilly, but I do know about that. Some FEMA chumps tried to get me to go into the camps but I just faded into the swamp until they quit coming around. You two look all right, you weren't in the camps were you?"

Michael looked at King, almost pleading for the big man to answer.

"Yes," King told him simply.

"Too many people? Lots of sickness?"

"Yes," the deep voice answered again.

"That's what I thought. Well boys, get your water, I'm going to drag this fish home and I'll be back. Do you want one? Four fish is probably more than I can eat before it goes bad," Carl asked.

"Sure," Michael said, his stomach rumbling in anticipation of something other than the travel food they had.

Even catfish sounded like a good meal, despite having lived off of it for months. The old man pulled the rope stringer out of the mouth of one of the largest fish, a bass, and handed it to Michael.

"Thank you," Michael said.

"You two have safe travels," Carl told them and walked up the embankment, the stringer of fish weighing him down and making him walk leaning to the side, the shotgun barely counter balancing the weight.

"That was…" Michael said.

"Weird," King finished.

§ § §

For two more days, they followed 59/20 south west towards Louisiana. According to the maps, it would be a little over a four hundred mile trip. Something that would have taken them six and a half hours if driving. But after a few days of walking, they'd come maybe fifty or sixty miles, if they were lucky.

"You want to try the Highway?" King asked, getting frustrated as well.

"We haven't walked across in a day or so, maybe it's not so choked up?" Michael said hopefully.

The EMP had happened on a Friday night, months and months ago. The surface streets didn't seem to be in as bad of shape as the highways, but people had left their cars where they had died. The electronics fried out on them. It had made the highway almost impassable for stretches and, although the NATO troops had been clearing roads and stretches of highway, it was closer to their base of operations. The nation itself still had huge areas clogged with dead cars.

"Maybe we get lucky and find something that

runs," King grinned.

"Glad I'm not the only one with sore legs," Michael said.

They both started up the embankment towards the asphalt and guard railing. It was a climb and they were wary as they went into the tall grass looking for snakes. Both were drenched in sweat as they crested the climb and stepped over the guard rail. As far as they could see, cars were parked, dead.

"We can walk for now," King said.

Michael nodded and followed the big man. What had worried both of them with this situation was how much cover there was between all the broken down cars. An ambush could be set up an hour ahead of time if conditions were good and somebody had been using binoculars to scout them out. The good news, was it also provided them with cover if somebody did try to ambush them. It was a win/lose situation, but their chances of finding supplies and moving faster in a straight line made it a little easier.

"So King, tell me about your time in the military," Michael said, breaking the silence.

"No," King told him, not unkindly.

"OK, what was it like for you growing up? Where were you from?" Michael asked.

"Born right here," King said, "Growing up wasn't fun."

"Wasn't fun? I mean, did you play football in school, girlfriend? Married?"

"You talk a lot," King said and kept moving.

BOYD CRAVEN

For an hour, Michael held his lip. They moved in and out of cars and, for a time, the highway wasn't raised as much as the surface streets. There was a median and, in the distance, they could see a dark shape sitting in the median, underneath an underpass.

"Scope that," King said pointing.

"Michael stopped and pulled out his binoculars.

He leaned against the hot metal of a car trunk and tried not to feel the burn against his elbows as he focused on the blob. He turned the focus knob and then saw what it was. An old tractor with brush cutters on both sides. It'd had been parked and left there, probably by whoever had the contract to cut the median and left it for the next time it was needed. Usually saved fuel that way.

"Tractor," Michael said, his elbows on fire.

"People?"

"Not that I can see. Here," Michael handed King the binoculars and rubbed his elbows.

"Come on kid," King said after a couple minutes, "I think we found ourselves a ride."

"A ri… wait, what?" Michael said as King started walking, whistling as he went.

§ § §

"I can work with this," King said, his face breaking into a rare grin.

"It's just an old tractor," Michael said, "can you hotwire it?"

CRIES OF THE WORLD

"Don't have to," King pulled a screwdriver from his backpack.

He opened the engine cowling and found the starting solenoid. Motioning Michael to stay back, King crossed the terminals with the screwdriver. Sparks flew and the old machine wheezed and then coughed black smoke as it fired up. King put his tool back and pushed his backpack into the cab, near where his feet would go.

"Not enough room for both of us inside. I'll teach you to drive this thing while you stand on the step there."

"It's loud, how are we going to hear anything?" Michael almost had to yell to hear himself over the din of the motor.

King pushed in a lever to idle it down and the noise dropped quite a bit.

"Won't go as fast that way, but we don't have to shout. Better on fuel. You're going to stand on the step here. Hold onto this, and you're my extra eyes and ears," King said, motioning for Michael to hand him his pack. He did, and the old carbine he got from his grandfather.

The ride started off bumpy but smoothed out when King was able to drive the tractor up onto the pavement. It wasn't fast travel, but it was faster than anything they had done it the past four days. Without a speedometer, they could only guess judging by the mile markers they were seeing.

"Hold on," Michael said, tapping King on the shoulder.

The big man idled down so it was barely running.

"What you see?" King asked, noting Michael's concerned look.

"Cars pushed together on the road. Nose to nose. Doesn't look like a wreck."

King hit the red stop button and the motor ground to a halt. It made ticking and pinging noises as the metal cooled. Michael was glassing the area when a glint of sunlight caught his attention. He was working to refocus on it when he caught sight of a gun barrel.

"Down," Michael yelled, jumping and landing hard on the ground.

Two shots rang out, hitting the bush hog on the right hand side, and King bailed out as well. With both of their hearts beating hard, they used the engine block and tires to hide behind.

"You get a good look at them?" King asked.

"No, just saw a barrel. I saw a flash of light and when I focused, I saw a barrel—" A shot rang out, kicking up the dirt a foot to the left of the front of the tractor, "and figured it was—"

"Scoped rifle. Good eyes, kid."

Every time King or Michael tried to get eyes on the roadblock, a shot would ring out.

"I hope they are running low on ammo," Michael said.

"Probably why whoever it is, is keeping us pinned down instead of rushing us?" Michael asked when it was clear that King wasn't going to answer.

CRIES OF THE WORLD

"Got an idea," King said, crawling between the two big rear tires.

A shot came dangerously close, but luckily King had just moved. Between the two large tires, King scoped the area out.

"Three guys. Rednecks. Looks like they're drinking beer and having fun," King, as always, was short and to the point.

"Want my rifle?" Michael asked.

"It's in the cab," King told him.

"Oh well, I can fix that!" Michael stood and took two quick steps and hopped onto the lower step to the cab, using the body of the tractor to cover his movements.

Multiple shots rang out, one of them blowing through the glass of the cab. The safety glass blew out and stuck to Michael's sweat soaked body in places. Reaching quickly, he snagged his grandfather's rifle and dropped to the ground, trying to roll behind the big tire in the back.

"Here," Michael yelled, tossing the gun butt stock first when he realized he couldn't reach King.

"You crazy, man. Crazy," King said, pulling the rifle to him.

The thunderous sound of shots on fully automatic broke the silence and Michael jumped, expecting the gunfire but it still scared him.

"One redneck down," King mumbled before firing again.

"Winged him, the rest are running. I only saw three, will keep looking." King said.

Michael hesitated a moment and peeked around the corner. No more shots came their way.

"Is it safe?" Michael asked.

"Think so," King said, crawling out from under the tractor.

Bits of grass and chaff stuck to him and he tried brushing it out of his hair, but it was fairly stuck. He handed Michael the rifle back and opened the motor cowling. He pulled the ignition wire off and then closed it up.

"What are we doing?" Michael asked.

"Going to see what those guys were doing." King said, moving to the highway quickly.

Michael followed and, using the cars as cover, they made their way slowly towards the ambush point. When they got to the cars that were nose to nose, Michael had to marvel. Starting low on the door three shots had gone through the door panel and one through the glass. Working slowly, they walked around where they found the body. The back of the car had matching holes, but judging by where the man was shot, at least of two of King's slugs had hit him.

It was a Mustang, and the glass or safety glass had blown out, covering him much the same way it did Michael. On the hood sat a partially torn open box of cans of Coors. Empties littered the ground.

"They was having a party, or camped out," King mused.

Michael started rifling the pockets of the dead man and came up with some .30/06 shells that

CRIES OF THE WORLD

would work in his gun. He pocketed them and went to the rifle. The stock was cracked and covered with duct tape. The barrel had a hank of rope tied to it in a makeshift sling. Even the scope was in poor shape. Michael emptied the gun and offered it to king who took it and using both of his big hands, swung the rifle by the stock.

He let go at the last second as the barrel hit, bending. When it came to rest, he got it and inspected his work. Smiling, he removed the bolt and threw the gun in the median.

"Never leave a working weapon at your back," King said.

"I'll remember that," Michael said.

He would too; he was going to just leave the gun there. But he realized that there was ammo in the world, and all it would take was for the other two to come up and feed it into the gun.

The rest of the hideout was pretty bare. There had been three cars, not two, pushed together. It was done in an almost U shape, if the cars were parked at ninety degree angles. The men must have gotten stupid after King had shot through the door panel, and stood to run. Blood splatter away from the corpse confirmed that King had indeed winged the other man, but no other supplies were found.

"Must be watching the road here. No supplies. Camped away from here. I'm worried these guys are going for help." King said.

"Me too. Want to take the tractor and go back to the small roads?"

"No," King said, motioning for them to start making their way back to the tractor.

Michael moved to cover him, and grinned when the big man grabbed the case of Coors with one big hand. They didn't move behind cover as before, but with a more hurried purpose. Michael slung his rifle over his shoulder when they got to the tractor. King put the ignition wire back and jumped it again and hopped in.

"Tap me if you see something. We're gonna hustle and it's going to be bumpy," King shouted as he idled up the motor.

Michael just nodded and hung on as the tractor took off, at almost twice the speed as it had before. It took both arms for Michael to hold on at times and the tractor was moving fast enough that he could feel the wind at his face, the sweat drying almost as soon as it tried to form on his skin. It was pleasant to be moving and moving at a decent clip, but it was punishing to his already sore body. Almost an hour and a half later, King idled back the tractor and then hit the stop button.

"What's up?" Michael asked, hopping off and stretching to get the kinks out of his cramping muscles.

"Need fuel." King told him, checking his side to make sure his pistol was still there.

That had almost become an unconscious thing for the two guys. It was like an old habit like checking your wallet. Make sure your gun is still seated in the holster well, and keep your water canteens full...

CRIES OF THE WORLD

Little things that marked how much the world had changed.

"Oh, uh… Where are we going to—"

"There," King pointed at a semi-tractor trailer sitting dead in the fast lane of 59/20 southbound.

King had parked the tractor very close to the semi, and Michael could immediately see his plan when he opened the cowling of the tractor and pulled out a length of plastic tubing from his pack.

"Syphon?" Michael asked.

"Yeah. Diesel don't taste good, so you gotta be careful," King said.

He dropped one end in the chromed fuel tank of the semi and Michael held the tube in place as he unrolled it to make sure it was long enough to go to the fuel tank in the tractor. It was, and had some room to spare, so King started sucking on one end of the hose. The fuel rose in the line, slowly and Michael could see the effort it was costing the big man. He must have been blowing out through his nose, but he never let go of the pipe until gravity took over and fuel started running towards the tractor.

King spat and pushed the end of the hose into the top of the fuel tank and used his shirt to wipe his tongue off.

"Wasn't fast enough," he complained.

Michael watched in awe as the fuel transferred with no pump. He had always thought there needed to be quite a bit of height difference for it to work and then he paused to consider it. Even though it wasn't a raised section of highway, the road surface was built up higher than the median. It'd have to be or it would flood. The fuel tank of the tractor was higher than the semi's tank, but there was enough of a difference in height to make it work. The hard part had been getting it started over such a long length of pipe.

"That's pretty cool. How long were you scouting for a spot to park and fuel up like this?" Michael said, proud he'd figured it out.

"Half an hour. It was this one or get fuel by hand," King told him.

"We were running close to empty?"

"Just a heartbeat away. Road gear moves you fast, but it's a pig for fuel."

They were silent until King told Michael to pull his end of the hose up. He recapped the semi's tank and held the hose up as instructed until all of it went into the tank of the tractor. They finished the refueling and got the tractor started again. King once more let it go all out but, after another hour, Michael had to tap him to get his attention. King idled the tractor down hard, almost throwing Michael off.

When Michael didn't jump for cover, King gave him a curious glance.

"What's wrong?" King asked.

"Too much bouncing. My arms are cramping," Michael admitted, not wanting to sound like a wuss, but they'd been traveling fast and hard.

"Good, I gotta kill a tree," King mumbled,

CRIES OF THE WORLD

switching the engine off.

Michael groaned. The big guy had a sense of humor somewhere, but he could never tell with that James Earl Jones voice until after he thought about it. King dug out a small foldable shovel and Michael almost laughed. He wasn't joking.

"Woods over there. You want to wait here?" King said.

"As opposed to…?"

"Nothing. Just want to know where to look for you when I come back," King said.

"I'll be here."

King took off for the tree line that covered the west side of the highway, across the northbound lane. Michael took the opportunity to look around. No obvious threats - and then he saw the mile marker. They had been making good time! What had taken them days of walking was done in less than an hour. It was bone jarring, but they could cover the distance in a few days if they were lucky. Michael pulled out a worn map and tried to follow their progress and used a pencil stub to make a note on the map. So much ground covered, so much more to go.

Soon, he hoped to find Lukashenko and his mother. He'd only had the rumors to go on, but he'd heard it from King and from some of Lukashenko's men who'd surrendered early on and hadn't been killed. If his mother was still alive, she'd be at the facility, King had assured him. There wasn't anywhere else close by. Michael prayed his mother

71

hadn't been abused like so many of the women in the camps and, with his father dead, it'd be up to him to watch after her. Protect her. Deep, dark thoughts clouded his vision and it was footsteps that finally brought him out of his daydream of revenge.

Michael spun, bringing his rifle to ready. King was making his way across the northbound lanes.

"Something spook you?" King called.

"You."

"I know I'm big and ugly, but don't shoot, white boy!" King joked, and Michael was for sure it was a joke this time.

They both chuckled as King made it to him.

"This time, you can drive," King said, "you ready?"

"Yeah," Michael said after hesitating, "Just don't steer it hard like a car, or it can tip?"

"Yup. I'll start her up." King said.

CHAPTER 6

THE HOMESTEAD, KENTUCKY

The man was let go. He truly didn't know anything. After being grilled for two days he'd finally cracked. It disgusted Duncan at how little the man knew, but he did give up the frequency that the Governor's men were using. With the right equipment, they should be able to break the encryption and get in. All the man wanted was a chance to flee. He had claimed he was forced back into the service and, once he was there, he couldn't do much or say much to go against the flow. If he would have shown that he wasn't on board, the others in his squad would have turned on him, as most of them were merc's.

As the man left, walking in the opposite direction the Governor's men had come from both times, Blake asked Duncan, "Do you really think it's like that? They're all too scared to share their own opinions? This can't be the only guy who didn't want to fight. You heard him; as soon as the fighting started, he dropped his gun and rolled under the truck. Pretty much matches up with Corrinne's accounting as well."

"There's always people who refuse to fight in a war not of their choosing," Duncan told him.

Blake thought on that. Silverman and some of his troops had left the Governor's control. Maybe they weren't the only ones who felt that what was going on was unlawful. If they could crack that frequency, Blake knew that Sandra would talk to them. Maybe it would even help to prevent another massacre. A twig snapped, bringing everyone to a halt and they waited silently. A rustle of leaves, louder than a deer would make, alerted them to somebody moving nearby.

"Corinne, any movement from the roads?" Sandra asked.

"Negative, other than the guy you sprung loose, I don't see anything."

Something prickled Sandra's Spidey senses and she shouted a warning, and dropped prone the same time her father and Blake did. Wood exploded right where her head would have been as the bullet hit the tree behind where she was just standing.

"Sniper fire," Sandra said into the mic before dropping it and reaching for her M4.

She waited and then heard another sharp report, but it hit somewhere deeper into the woods. One more shot and then her radio crackled, "Ma'am, sniper down. Figure there's two more in his team. Guarantee you they're all armed," one of Sgt. Smith's men said.

"Should we sweep them up?" Duncan asked.

"I don't know. I don't want to stay pinned down for hours if they have left, but I don't want to play cat and mouse with a sniper team," Sandra spat, angry in a way Blake hadn't seen her before.

Everyone stayed down until a string of automatic fire disturbed the silence. More than one weapon was firing and Duncan demanded a sitrep for whomever was out there. The gunfire stopped and Corinne came back on the radio.

"Situation is normal. All F'd Up," she said with a giggle.

"Darn kids," Duncan snarled, "just when you want them to be serious they go and—"

"Caught two men in ghillie suits trying to sneak out. Told them to stop. They didn't, and raised their rifles so…"

"Two less bad guys?" Blake asked.

"Two less bad guys." Corinne confirmed through the speaker.

"Sandra, why don't you and Blake head uphill. I'm going to link up with the perimeter guards and see what had been set up. Counter sniper team probably has their hide all marked off now," Duncan said.

"Dad, you know I should be out there on point and—"

"You're pregnant with my grandbaby," Duncan said and that shut her objections down.

"Rats. No wonder you always preached safe sex," Sandra grumped and Blake laughed when Duncan turned five shades of red. It was either embarrassment or anger, but Blake wasn't going to stick around and find out. They worked their way back to the end of the lane where Blake's real driveway started.

"Why do you think they were there?" Blake asked.

"To shoot somebody," Sandra said softly.

"But who?" Blake asked.

"You or me. It's the only thing that makes sense." Sandra said.

"We have to delegate some of this stuff out more, you know." Blake said taking her hand in his.

"That just makes them a target," she said angrily, meaning the folks who lived and worked at the Homestead.

"Probably safer than we are, right now."

"Probably. Now we just have to figure out if we need to hit back at the Governor, and figure out how to keep his men out of our area." Sandra told him, pulling her hand free.

"We couldn't keep the cannibal out," Blake said after a pause, remembering how Ken Robertson almost ruined their lives.

"He wasn't human," Sandra told Blake, "He was just some sort of creepy lizard who crawled out of the muck somewhere."

CRIES OF THE WORLD

"Nice visual."

"Thanks."

§ § §

It had been quiet, too quiet. Three days after the sniper was found, they finally cracked the code for the encrypted frequency so their scrambler units could broadcast more than the usual gibberish. There were requests for Collins to report in on multiple occasions and, on the fourth day, they heard about a unit that was going to be put together to come to the Homestead. They referred to it by name, 'The Homestead', and they were planning on finding out what kept happening to their men and supplies.

"I wonder if they think they joined us?" Blake asked.

"Probably." Sandra told him distractedly, Chris working on a coloring book at her feet.

"Sounds like a mixed unit plus some armor," David said, cutting into the conversation.

"Really? What do they have?" Sandra asked.

"Sounds like their military holdouts have some MRAPS or APCs of sort, maybe even some assault vehicles. Mixed bag. Things aren't organized by the sounds of it, and none of the usual peeps on the radio sound military." David told them.

"Well, there's a few," Patty said turning to them, "but not many. Most military over the radio don't give themselves ridiculous nicknames, do they?"

Patty asked Sandra.

"You'd be surprised. But here in the States? No, I don't think that's all that common." Sandra said.

"What do we do?" Blake asked them both.

"We make a plan, then execute it," Duncan said.

"Now that we're on their frequency, can't we just try talk to them? I really don't want to make this any worse than it is and kill a bunch of innocent people," Blake told them.

"I know, hun," Sandra said, putting her arms around his middle.

Blake smiled. The baby bump easily showed on her slender frame, and it was pressed into the small of his back. Soon he knew, he'd be able to feel the baby moving around. Another month, and he would feel what only Sandra could.

"Right now, they don't know we cracked their frequency. It might be the tactical advantage we need," Duncan said.

"Wait a second… The unit is being led by a Sgt. Silverman? Yeah, that's what I thought I heard." Patty said.

Sandra stiffened.

"He said they were bugging out, that they weren't going to attack. I wonder…" Sandra started to say.

"You think he held out to snag what he could, or do you think he was trying to pull one over on us?" Blake asked Sandra.

"We won't have much time to react if we don't prepare now. What do we have that can take out an

APC?" Duncan asked rhetorically, already knowing the answer.

"Do like we did last time. Fire down on them with mortars from a distance or blow up some of your Oklahoma City bomber mix. We still have a ton of that stuff just sitting out at the various farms waiting to be used," Sandra said with a grin.

"We could also use thermite grenades," Sgt. Smith said, joining the conversation, as he walked in from outside.

"Well, let's listen to the rest of the chatter and start making plans to take them out if they are in fact coming after us," Duncan said.

Blake was soaking it all up, and his mind was whirling. He didn't like the thought of the Governor sending troops against them. It would make it three times that he'd sent men to come and take what was theirs, or to just outright kill and murder Blake and Sandra. What else were those forty some odd troops for? Definitely not a peace mission. The only thing result would be a horrific loss of life - and give further military equipment to the Homestead.

Sandra's handheld crackled and she put the earpiece in and said, "Go," and smiled. She grabbed a piece of paper and rattled off some numbers, while doing some math on the pad. She wrote down the response and then nodded.

"Silverman, I hear you loud and clear, over," she said, handing her handset to David.

"Plug this into the speakers, would ya?"

"But don't we want to listen—" Patty was saying.

"Got it."

They exchanged numbers, confirming it was a legit call.

"Sandra, Silverman here. Took longer to bug out than anticipated. Only way to get the families out safely was to wait until we had transport and when the last two transports didn't come back... you wouldn't know about that, would you? Over."

"No clue. Maybe they took those transports and headed to Mexico. Rumors are, parts of it has power still and the tequila flows like wine.... Over."

"Ha, ha! It's ok, they were pretty much scum. Dirt bags that had been let out of prison or the dishonorable discharges that were forced back into the service. Not one of them had a lick of discipline. I had nothing to do with them and told the Governor it was a dumb idea to send that many for a brute force attack. I'm hoping everyone there is ok. Over."

"Oh, we're fine," Sandra said, "What pissed me off was the sniper team that was trying to take out me and Blake. That one I will claim. They failed and we left them out for the dogs and coyotes. Over."

The line was silent a long time, and when Silverman spoke up again, his voice was full of sadness.

"Must be the Governor's Black Ops team. I don't know much about them, but if he'd sent my guys in, they would have faded into the woodwork and waited for us to show up. If he sent those guys in... He must want you pretty badly. Over."

CRIES OF THE WORLD

"What do we have to do to have no more teams come after us? How do I trust that you aren't working both sides against the middle, over?" Sandra spoke aloud her fear, that Silverman was tired of the Governor, but was using the Homestead to whittle down his forces.

"If I was working both sides against the middle, I wouldn't leave. I'd just sit back and wait," Silverman said, his voice starting to crackle over the speaker, "As far as the Governor, I don't know. You can talk to him about peace. I doubt it'd work. Probably going to have to make it a more personal chat or take the fight to him. Over."

"Damn," Blake swore, "That's exactly what I don't want. What do we do if he gets his hands on a tank? An Apache? We can't fight that, not with what we've got."

"We actually can," Sandra said, "but the losses would be unacceptable. I think we have to talk to the men and not the man himself."

"How would that work?" Blake asked.

Sandra told him. About halfway through, Duncan started nodding and smiling.

§ § §

The teams split up. Several ambush points were marked and armed with the ANFO barrels. Since there was armor involved, they went full load and buried all but the lids. They might not be able to punch the armor, but the blast would be enough to flip or throw the APC over, making them useless in case Silverman was lying. The Homestead became a hive of activity, preparing for yet another threat, but in two days, when Silverman left out, they were ready.

"You going to listen in while I mess with the troops?" Sandra asked Blake.

"I should, but I don't know. Chris has been wanting me to take him out and, after listening to that last massacre, I don't want to... you know, in case he was lying," Blake admitted.

"Hey, if this stuff didn't bug you... You wouldn't be the man you are." Sandra said.

"You just seem so good at not letting it show," Blake admitted, "Except when you're sleeping."

"What's that supposed to mean?" she asked, her eyes twinkling in mischief.

"Well, you talk. Mumble. I mean, I didn't know you loved chocolate milkshakes as much as you seem to," Blake smiled.

"Chocolate milkshakes? Who doesn't?" Sandra said getting close to Blake, her hands threatening to tickle.

"Hey, I can figure out a way to make some." Blake smiled and pulled Sandra close, holding her arms to her sides.

If it were anybody else, Blake would have been disabled, on the ground bleeding, but Sandra allowed it and smiled as he pulled her into a warm hug.

"Good, you figure that out with Chris, and I'm

CRIES OF THE WORLD

going to play psy-ops with Boss Hogg's men. But chocolate milkshakes would be something I'd want you to make a ton of, especially when we get ice for the ice house going."

"Love you babe," Blake said kissing the top of her head and letting her go.

"Don't be gone too long. If things go south…"

"Oh, we're probably going to head to edge and start setting some big snares and then I'll poke through the barn for something to make a big tub. I think I have something in mind actually…"

Sandra started laughing.

"What?" Blake asked.

It wasn't Sandra who answered, it was Patty who was also grinning.

"When you put your mind to it, you usually do something amazing like a Junkyard Warrior… but if you can pull off chocolate ice cream? I think Sandra's going to have to beat the ladies off with a stick," Patty said, batting her eyes at Blake in a teasing fashion.

"Oh no, this Junkyard Warrior is mine," Sandra said smiling, "besides, he's going to get me some smoked pork for the baby, right?"

"You got it."

Blake and Chris left as Sandra keyed up the radio.

"So where are we going?" Chris asked.

"Well, we still have a ton of wild hogs, and more deer than you could shake a stick at. I'm going to set out a bunch of snares to see if we can get some,"

Blake said, slowing his pace to allow his adopted son to keep pace easily.

"Can't you just shoot them?"

"Sure, but if everyone from the Homestead went hunting, there would be a ton of accidents. This way, we leave the snares out and check them later on, or tomorrow morning, until we catch something. Then we put it down if it's not dead. Usually it's dead. Then we can take down the rest of the snares when we get enough." Blake told the little man.

"So by putting out five or six snares, that's like five or six hunters when there's only two of us?"

Blake was blown away by the little man's reasoning. He was close to six, and had just grasped the concept of what Sandra would have called a force multiplier.

"Yes, exactly," he said, ruffling Chris's hair, messing it up some.

§ § §

They put out seven sets and wandered back to the barn, not the root cellar, nor the secret barracks, but the half organized riot of materials and junk from an older era. It hadn't been the first time he'd gone through the rusted appliances to build something, but it was an easy build out for him. He removed the drum from a dryer with Chris's help and put that on the floor. He then went looking for something that would hold the cream and a way to stir it.

CRIES OF THE WORLD

The old butter churn he found was too tall for the drum, but he kept the lid, which had a hole already through the middle. Now to find something for the lid to sit on, and something to stir with. The wooden handle of the butter churn might work in a pinch. It looked like years of use had left it smooth and sliver free. Still, he kept looking until he found an old water bath canner. Chris was dancing with happiness as the two of them almost fit together perfectly.

"What do you think?" Blake asked Chris.

"What is it?" a small voice asked and Blake turned to find that in his mad hunt through the leavings from an older and gentler time, he'd drawn an audience.

"Well," Blake said looking at the young boys and girls, mixed with quite a few of the Homestead's grownups not on chores, watching him, "it's going to be an ice cream maker when we can get some ice. I sort of remember how to do it, so I'm going to make it and hope for the best."

"Ice cream!" The words buzzed through the crowd and it wasn't long before word had spread.

It started off with Chris being Blake's only helper, but soon he had three adults helping and scavenging for materials for him.

"Would an insulated box help?" Curt asked, keeping half an eye on his daughter Melissa, and Bobby.

"Yeah," Blake mumbled, "That was going to be the next thing on my list actually," he smiled at the room at large. Suddenly kids and adults alike were scrambling to help.

"So Blake," Bobby said walking up hand in hand with Melissa, "How do you make Ice cream?"

"It's pretty simple. You put heavy cream in the middle tub here, add your flavoring... vanilla, chocolate, fruit juice or whatever. Then you fill the outer tub with ice and salt. The salt lowers the temperature as the ice melts a bit and you crank some sort of stirrer. Pretty easy stuff actually," Blake said, hoping his understanding of the how was accurate.

"That sounds too easy," Melissa said.

"It really is. But, before we get cream, we have to have a cow or two."

"That's on the list," Martha said from amidst a pile of junk.

"Hey Martha, I didn't know you were up here," Blake said.

"When I heard there was ice cream to consider, I traded my shift with one of the younger girls. Besides, there's got to be some heifers out there still who are in milk, and the kids here could really use it," Martha said, coming out from a pile of old rusted junk holding a large scrap of insulation.

"Oh nice! That should fit around the outer tub well!"

So went the afternoon. A box was built around the old tub, and it had insulation all around. It didn't look as ridiculous as Blake thought it would. The handle and spinner ended up being the old churn

CRIES OF THE WORLD

handle as nothing else would fit. They decided to just be careful and test it before going on a search for something in stainless steel. All in all, it would work and, with the springhouse complete, they could keep milk cool for a time, enough to allow the cream to separate. If only Martha could find him some cows…

CHAPTER 7

MICHAEL & KING

Two days of travel and refueling had made them both tired and sore. The bone jarring ride of the tractor had become almost painful to them, but they had covered a great deal of distance. They'd had to refuel two to three times a day, but the breaks were longer and longer as their bodies needed time to heal up.

"Want to spend a day or so here?" King asked, looking at the place they'd stopped at.

"Not out in the open…" Michael said and then laughed at himself.

They hadn't been. They'd pulled the ignition wire off the tractor at night time and made a crude camp in the woods. They didn't know how the terrain was going to be and Michael complained that if they only had google maps with satellite

CRIES OF THE WORLD

view...

"Don't know what that is, kid. Google was a new thing when I went to jail," King told him when he mentioned it.

"See it's on the website, you could pick your directions and zoom..."

"Kid, when computers work again I'll have you show me," King grumped and Michael stopped and nodded, grinning.

It felt weird to have King with him at times. When he stayed with John, he felt close to him, more like they were on even footing. Somehow with King, it felt more like he did when he was with his father on long hunting or fishing trips. That thought sent a pang of guilt and regret through his system. Still, King was treating him like a son, even if his words were short and he was abrupt. It was just his nature.

"You coming?" King asked.

"Yup."

They gathered their supplies and headed into the brush, pushing their way until the woods opened up, with the larger trees forming a perfect canopy against the hot sun.

"Let's rest today and tomorrow. Get back on the road the day after. Sound good?" King asked.

"Sure. I've got enough water for that."

"Me too," King said, "But I think we can find something close. I remember the other night you told me about the trick the kid did with the yo-yo; will you show me?"

BOYD CRAVEN

Michael proudly showed King away from the camp over a game trail. Tie off the yo-yo, and pull the length of line out until you were where you wanted the hoop of the snare to be. Michael then took a long steel leader and put the line through the swivel snap, making a hoop. He then hooked it up to the swivel on the yo-yo's line and used sticks pressed into the ground to push the animal towards the opening that was trapped. Michael was just finishing things up when King asked him something.

"What holds the loop open? It's falling down all the time," King asked.

"Grass," Michael told him.

He tied a six inch piece of grass loosely where he wanted the loop to be. He demonstrated by putting his wrist into the loop and pulling. The grass ripped and the snare slipped over his hand easily. King laughed at the kid's ingenuity and they reset it. In all, they set out five sets before almost stumbling into a small pool of water.

"We're in luck." King said, bending over until his nose was almost on the surface of the water.

"Smells fresh. Spring?" King asked.

Michael shrugged; most of his experiences with water were rivers and lakes. Not a random ten foot diameter body of water in the middle of nowhere. Still, there were frogs at the edges and Michael looked for fish. Not seeing any, he followed King back, using his knife to hack away at the bark, always on the same side.

CRIES OF THE WORLD

That night, they didn't have a fire and laid out under the canopy of the trees. It was silent and, in a world gone slightly crazy, it was comforting not to have the loud din of civilization. Michael didn't even miss it. He was falling asleep when King spoke up.

"When I was a kid, I was always picked on. Segregation was done and over with, but the South is the South, where ignorance is accepted. I wanted nothing more than to escape and go live somewhere else. My parents were poor share croppers. I grew up on the same farm they did, but we had modernized equipment. They always knew when I came home bloody that it was the kids at school. I tried to get good grades, but I kept getting thrown out for fighting.

"Then one day, a recruiter came to our school. I was maybe, 8th grade? I don't remember. Told us all about the Army. Finish school, join up. Travel the world, get a better education. It sounded good to me and that was what I did. I worked hard in school, lifted weights hoping to play for the Crimson Tide if the Army thing fell through and life was good. When those two assholes kicked in my door, my life changed. I assume John shared that part with you?"

Michael looked at nodded.

"The Army stuff, I don't talk about that. It was uglier than this world we're in now. I don't talk about that to nobody."

"OK," Michael said, awed by the speech.

King wasn't known to be a big talker, even in

prison, but he'd been opening up more and more. One word sentences were becoming full sentences with fleshed out thoughts. Michael had no doubt that the big man was smart, deadly smart... and as he thought on that he realized that he was also guarded. His thoughts, his past, his emotions. Maybe that's what prison and murder do to a man.

Michael had to check himself there; he'd killed also. He felt horrible about it. Brett and Linny's father, the man who'd tried to steal his bike and strand him in the woods, was the first of several.

"Figured you should know. Never know about tomorrow." King told him, then rolled over and seemingly fell asleep instantly.

"Wow," Michael said to himself.

§ § §

Dawn was breaking and King was starting to wake when Michael heard thrashing down the trail. He pulled his .45 and stood on shaky feet as the adrenaline pumped through his veins.

"What is it?" King asked, rubbing his eyes.

"Think we have breakfast," Michael said, a little breathless from the excitement.

"Good. I'm hungry."

That was the running joke, King was always hungry and most of his pack contained food. Nothing gourmet, but more along the lines of MREs and food bars he'd gotten from John before departing. The amount of food the huge man could consume was… huge.

The first two traps were triggered, but no animals were in them. He let King reset them both. The third one contained a flopping grouse, somehow snared by its leg. It kept trying to fly away but the line pulled it back. King walked up and grabbed it, twisting its head off and unhooking it. Michael smiled and started to set that one to rights as he watched the big man take the skin by the neck and pull. Feathers and entrails came steaming out in one big yank. From start to finish it took him less than a minute.

Michael stood there awestruck.

"Told you, grew up on a farm," King smiled, the white of his teeth shockingly bright.

The next snare didn't have anything, but the last one had a fat rabbit. It had strangled, the wire around its neck. Even in death it had been pulling away from the line. King watched as Michael cleaned it and they both walked back to camp, their stomachs rumbling for fresh meat. Michael laid out a quick fire pit dug into the ground and they used a 12x12 grill grid they had taken. They cut sticks to lay across the corners of the pit, to help hold the grate level. The sticks would eventually burn, but not before the cooking was done.

Michael watched as King used a jackknife to cut the cleaned grouse in half and throw both sides of them on the grate to start cooking.

"Wish we could change the height some," King said after a minute.

"I can scare up some rocks?" Michael asked as the fire leapt towards the grouse.

"Naw, this is good. Might be a little overdone when it's ready. Should have waited for coals, but I was hungry," King smiled at Michael a little sheepishly.

"Me too," Michael dug through his pack and came out with two treasured items. Salt and pepper shakers, each in their own Ziploc baggies.

"Use some of that?" King asked.

Michael nodded and handed them over. King liberally sprinkled both over the grouse before turning the bird over with his fingers and repeating the operation. When it was done, Michael threw the pieces of chopped up rabbit on the grate. As that cooked, King handed him half a bird.

Surprisingly, the meat was pretty good. Not like chicken, but flavorful. A lot better than the MREs or the canned food he'd been eating. When the rabbit was done, they split the food again. Michael couldn't finish his half, and gave the rest to his new found friend. King ate it gratefully and, when the fire finally died down, he pushed all the bones into the fire after removing the grate. Kicking the dirt back in the hole, he laid back contentedly.

"Good times," King said.

"Yeah, I just wish I knew for sure whether my Mom was OK." Michael said.

"She'll have to be, or we'll burn the joint down," King said simply.

They took turns keeping an eye out and napping.

CRIES OF THE WORLD

Something that Michael had learned early on, was that a body can't operate at peak performance when fear and uncertainty saps your energy. Soon, you lose your edge, and the only way he'd found to fix it was sleeping. A person couldn't operate the way they did when the world was simple, and all you worried about was getting grounded for feeling up the chief's daughter…

A snapping twig had King on his feet immediately. He held a finger to his lips, and Michael nodded. They grabbed their packs and faded back into the woods as a figure slowly worked itself into the small clearing. Michael tensed as he crouched, the old carbine ready to go. King pulled his .45 and waited. At that point, moving fast to escape would make noise, noise they couldn't afford.

"… I could smell cooking and fire."

"Yes, yes, but I must get to the Louisiana facility. I don't have time to waste on your fruitless search for—"

"Sir, with due respect, I'm not leaving a raider to ambush me at my back. Be silent and let my men work," the voices were Eastern European, and Michael swore he recognized one voice in particular.

King motioned for Michael to get even lower. Luckily, the extra clothing they'd taken was from the soldiers at the last FEMA camp. They were decked out in the same CAMO as the men combing the woods. Maybe they could slip out in plain sight? They'd leave the snares behind, but not having a shootout was higher in Michael's priorities than the yo-yos.

"I am the ranking officer here. You have no business talking to me—" Lukashenko said, now visible to Michael and King.

Michael took the safety off the gun, his hands starting to shake. King put a comforting arm on Michael's shoulder. The anger, the hatred… The man in front of him had killed his Father and sent his Mother away to God knows what. Michael's finger tensed, but he waited as the man spoke.

"Comrade," the man Lukashenko had been talking to pulled a knife and held it under the officer's throat, "You are a prison warden. I am a true soldier. I did not get my commission because of family ties. You make more noise and get us discovered or killed, I'll cut your fucking throat and leave you out here. Are we clear?"

"You can't… when central command… You'll hang," Lukashenko shouted.

Shots rang out from further back in the woods than Michael and King had camped. Voices screamed warnings, and the man holding Lukashenko at knifepoint went through with his promise, ending half of Michael's mission in one bloody swipe. Michael almost cried out at the loss, but buried his head in the soil for a moment. The man who had killed Lukashenko pointed further into the woods, 180 degrees way from where Michael and King were hiding. The direction the shots had come from. They took off, hardly giving

CRIES OF THE WORLD

the area more than a look. Gone. Half the reason for this bloody trip and he'd been robbed of his revenge.

Slowly, King motioned for Michael to stand and reached over, clicking the safety on the pistol held by the shaking man-child. He approached Lukashenko, noticing that the blood was still flowing. He wasn't dead. King used his foot to roll him over. Lukashenko tried mouthing something, but blood bubbled out of his mouth and he jerked a couple of times before dying. His last sight was Michael and King, two people he remembered well.

"Hurry," King said and they moved in the direction the men came in.

"Steal their truck?" Michael asked.

"Stealing will get you put in jail, kid," King said stone faced.

Considering the timing and history, that struck Michael as funny and he had to bite his cheek in order to not laugh out loud. They paused to look around and found the APC almost immediately. It was parked a quarter of a mile away. Barely able to make it out, Michael pulled the binoculars and handed them to King. Standing beside it, a man was smoking a cigarette. The men must have driven north to pick up Lukashenko when they either smelled or saw the smoke from the small fire.

"You know how to drive one of those things?" Michael asked.

"Nope. Lucky, that one is just a transport. No guns. Gun ports, but no big guns like John used."

"Why is that good?" Michael whispered as they moved parallel through the woods.

"If there was guns, a gunner would be left behind, probably more than one. Then the driver. If they have the same basic squad size and no guns, there should only be the one man. I'm going to get in close and take him out silently and check inside."

"How are you going to get close?" Michael asked.

"We wear the same uniforms," King admitted, showing Michael he'd had similar thoughts to the one's he'd had earlier.

"No way. I didn't see a big black dude with them. They'd shoot you on sight if they saw you in that uniform."

"That's racist," King said deadpan and then smiled when Michael looked at him in shock, "Kidding. You're the same size as them, but I don't know if you'd be—"

'I can do it," Michael said stoically.

"Good. Hand me your rifle and pack. Don't talk if he calls out to you. If things go south I'll hit them from afar and come up with a new plan," King said, checking the rifle over.

"Ok," Michael said, feeling for his Colts and then checking the small of his back for the bowie knife.

§ § §

CRIES OF THE WORLD

The beauty of the plan was that people see what they expect to see. The soldier gave Michael one glance and then went to the other side of the APC. Michael closed the hundred foot distance quickly, without jogging or running. He got close and heard water running and saw the growing puddle from the side of the APC. The man was taking a break to urinate. Knowing he had a second or two, he glanced in the gun port and saw the interior empty and lit from the open hatch above.

"You hurt?" the man asked, his accent so slight that Michael couldn't make out what it was.

"Nyet," Michael said, knowing his accent and language would give him away.

He already had his .45s in his hands when the man stepped around the corner, his eyebrows raised. They almost touched his forehead as he looked into the bores of the handguns.

"You're not one of us," the man whispered in barely broken English.

King broke cover from the woods and ran up, his arms laden with gear.

"Zip tie?" Michael asked.

"Let's conk him and boogie," King said, dropping the gear and cracking his knuckles.

"He knows the way, I'm sure. Plus, he can drive this."

King grinned. The man blanched under the giant's smile. He only trembled a little when King disarmed him, even removing the thin bladed stiletto in his left boot.

"You're going to drive, got it?" King said, holding the man at gunpoint while Michael threw the gear in the hatch.

The soldier nodded.

"You turn, or if you run or try to attack the kid inside, we'll splatter your guts all over this fine piece of equipment."

Again, the toothy grin unnerved the man and he scrambled up into the APC like the devil was after him. The man had no idea how close to death he had been. If he'd kept looking at Michael, he would have made him out to not be one of theirs and Michael's knife would have had to come into play. The man's weak bladder gave Michael ten seconds to check out the APC, and had given the man a chance to live. If he listened. It was luck, Michael was sure.

"We closing this?" King gestured towards the hatch, and Michael shrugged.

King closed it anyways and took in the darkened surroundings. The man was already sitting in the driver's seat, half turned to look at them.

"How far are we from the Louisiana Camp?" Michael asked, a .45 loosely aimed at the soldier.

"A day's travel," the man stuttered.

"What should we call you?" King asked.

"Chad, sir. My American name," he stammered.

"Chad it is. Take us that way, Chad, and you better be forthcoming with your answers," King said, pulling a wicked knife out of his pack, unsheathing it.

CRIES OF THE WORLD

"Answers?" Chad asked, trying not to gulp.

"Yeah, cuz you're about to sing like a bird. One way or another," King said, grinning again.

Michael realized that the toothy grin intimidated the man more than the knife or the gun. King would obviously get the information, but Michael wanted to drive the vehicle if they had to kill and dump the man. He started studying and watching how things worked as the APC rumbled back to life and left the area.

§ § §

Hours later, King directed Chad to pull off the road into a park. Chad backed the APC into the tree line, pushing over small saplings and crunching dead branches under the heavy tires.

"You think he's telling the truth?" Michael asked King, aware that Chad was still sitting next to him.

"Yeah. I don't trust him, but I think he told us everything he could. He isn't high enough up to know shit that's important, but he told us the truth," King said.

"I did, I swear," Chad insisted, nervous but not panicking.

Chad had told them that the camp was set up differently than the Alabama one. It wasn't as heavily guarded, because the port was so close. They required workers and the men there were often removed in large groups to go work at the port, a refinery or something else that just took brute force

101

labor. The women and kids, according to Chad, were held in the same buildings and the horrors of Alabama were not a common thing. He told them that rape or sexual favors were non-existent there. With some luck, they could free them without a great loss of life.

The radio crackled and Chad looked at them, a question on his lips.

"Any bet it's him again?" King asked.

"No bet," Chad said.

"Chad, report," a bored voice said, "you're not at the pickup point,"

The soldier had been calling for an hour. Evidentially Chad had been used to waiting all day for the team to do a mission and, by the sounds of it, they had Intel that made them think there were people deeper into the woods than Michael and King had been. A very lucky turn of events; the whole day had been lucky really.

"If we don't let him talk to the man, are they going to radio base next?" Michael asked.

"Talk to the man," King said, motioning with the knife, "one screw up and I cut your throat and throw you out the hatch.

One other thing the man had told them, was that he was conscripted when he was younger and the American Crisis had his government activating him and sending him with a mixed bag of NATO men. He claimed he didn't want to come. It was a sad story that had heard before and sounded like some of the men at the FEMA camp they had just left.

CRIES OF THE WORLD

"Chad here, where you been? Over?"

"You're not at the pickup. What happed? Can you do pickup now? Over."

"No, the APC started to overheat. I went back a few miles for water. Still too hot to crack the cap. Will let you know when I can get back to you. My orders were to keep radio silence while you were out on mission…"

"You didn't hear our first 10 calls to you? Over." the voice asked incredulously.

The same voice belonging to the man who'd cut Lukashenko's throat.

"No, perhaps it is these hills or the garbage in the sky from the EMP? Over."

There was a long pause and then, "Understood. Keep us informed. We will start walking to you. What way you travel, north? Over."

"Yes, travel four miles north to creek. Over."

"See you soon. Out."

Chad had broken out into a hard sweat and he wiped at his face. They were not north of them, in fact they were most of the day's drive south of them. The radio reception was shockingly clear for the distance they'd traveled.

"These things overheat much?" King asked.

"Piece of shit Russian surplus," Chad spat and then laughed as the other two busted up as well.

CHAPTER 8

"A re they turning?" Corrine asked over her coms.

"Negative, coming right down the road, over." A spotter said.

"Try hailing them?" Sandra's voice broke in.

"No, figured I'd let you," the spotter's voice said.

"Any towed artillery?" Sandra asked.

"No, just heavy machine guns on the MRAP. Over."

"Damn," Sandra swore to herself. She keyed up the private frequency she used with Silverman. "Sgt. Silverman, do you read me?"

"Loud and clear, over." The reception was very clear, he must be close.

"If that is you coming down the highway towards us, kindly stop what you're doing. Over,"

CRIES OF THE WORLD

Sandra said.

"We're now an hour south of you, over."

Sandra swore even louder.

"Ok, the Governor must have sent out a second squad. It's about to be toast. Over," she said.

"Wait one," Silverman asked and Sandra waited for him to come back on the horn, "That isn't ours. Boss Hogg, as you called him, must have gotten wind of our defection. I don't know if they're coming for you or us. Over."

"Forward Observer, you copy?" Sandra said into the handset, changing frequencies.

"I copy. Over."

"Start calling the shots and bring down the fire," Sandra said.

They had repositioned the towed artillery that Sgt. Smith had brought to almost the end of the lane. It was a flat area with no obstructions. They could reach out miles and miles away if they could get the timing right. It may not take it out entirely, but it could disable it. With a WP round, they could cook the drivers alive on the inside. It was the ugly reality of war, and they could only hope that the vehicles coming their way didn't have heavy guns. In this instance, they didn't, just machine guns. The Governor's men must have thought it'd be an easy thing to do, but they were about to learn a painful lesson.

Sandra could hear the mortar teams firing and then an explosion ripped through the air. Things fell silent.

"Sitrep?" Sandra demanded.

"Two MRAPS on their side. The rest of the troops are bugging out. I repeat, bugging out. We got lucky boss."

"Wait one, survivors," Duncan said, "let's round them up, ladies."

Duncan kept Sandra abreast of what was going on as her squad pulled eight shell shocked men from the armored vehicles. When the blast had gone off, they hadn't timed the dynamite fuse properly. The majority of the explosion went off in front of them but the concussion had pushed them over on their side. When the artillery had begun hitting the ground, the AP rounds mixed with HE took out the next two vehicles. Problem was, the timing was off and they'd been aiming at the armor, not the trucks.

"That could have been a lot worse," David said to Patty, listening to two different conversations with the radio equipment going.

"A lot worse, sounds like we got really lucky," Patty agreed.

§ § §

The explosion and deep sounds of the mortars going off was lost on Blake and most of the Homestead while they were tearing through the barn, but when they were done, Blake went in search of his wife to share the news that ice cream would be a definite maybe soon. All it had to do was get cold enough to freeze outside.

He considered making forms for making large blocks of ice to use, but decided to wait and see if the cache of five gallon buckets they were finding everywhere would work better.

Sandra found him and Chris walking back to the house to start on dinner. Her face was solemn and a little drawn from worry.

"How'd it go?" Blake asked.

"We, uh… well, we got lucky. We aren't going to keep getting lucky like this, though." Sandra said, "I'm kind of scared of what they're going to do next."

"Think I should talk to Davis?" Blake asked.

"I think it'd be a good idea. He thinks of you as the leader and head of this… and you are. But he wouldn't respect me or take me serious. Because… you know…" Sandra stammered.

"Because you're a woman and he's an old school pig?" Blake asked her.

She nodded, "Plus, I don't want to keep having to do…"

Sandra broke down and started to cry. Blake knew it must have been bad, but if they'd suffered any causalities she would have told him first. Probably a lot more dead men, he thought, but they'd belong to the other side.

"Chris and I were going to get something to eat. You want to come with us, or do you want some time alone?"

"I need some time alone to process. I told everyone on the handsets that I was off for a bit, so they won't bug me. I'm set on the same frequency I used to contact Silverman. Find me there if you need me. I just need a quiet spot for a while."

Blake had seen every victory building up inside of her. A well of sorrow. He didn't know how she could deal with so much pain and death, even if it was strangers bent on hurting them, but she did. Maybe she needed time to decompress. Blake knew that he'd needed that as well, especially with the Homestead full of so many survivors.

"Ok, babe. I'll get a handset from the house and listen in, or if you want to listen while I talk to Boss Hogg..."

"I probably will. Love you, country boy," she said leaning in for a kiss.

"Love you too," Blake smiled, her kisses always having that effect on him.

"Me too!" Chris piped up and laughed as Sandra bent over and gave him a sloppy kiss on the forehead, blowing a raspberry at the end.

"Ewww, not fair!" he complained.

"Let's go bud, we're going to let Mom take her walk," Blake said, "Besides, I have to go make a fat man angry."

§ § §

Sandra wasn't the epic badass everyone held her up to be. In her own mind she was a young lady with a particular skill set. She hadn't had to use it much in the war, but she did have her own personal body

CRIES OF THE WORLD

count. It haunted her. She kept that bottled up, and even more so after the EMP took out the lights and power for much of the world. When Blake had first killed, she wanted to hold him close and lie and tell him it got easier.

Since John Davis rolled into town, they'd probably killed fifty or sixty men, and most of them were at her orders. Even the mop up operations she'd ordered had killed the people that might have made it with medical treatment. Every sermon her father gave, every face she remembered, was a stab of guilt in her body. She'd stayed strong for Blake and the baby, but she didn't want to go to pieces in front of everyone. Not because she was worried it would shatter the carefully crafted image she upheld for the sake of the Homestead, but because she didn't like for people to see her cry. It was her one mark of pride, and one that would get her into trouble.

The sound of compressed air releasing in a quick shot made Sandra jump and she felt a sharp stinging in her side, under her armpit. She pulled out a dart with a syringe. She could already feel the effects of the drug so she pulled out her handset and keyed it up.

"Blake, honey, I think we have a problem," she said her words coming out to a slur as she slumped to the ground unconscious.

§ § §

BOYD CRAVEN

Blake had been needling John Davis over his losses and trying to convince him to cease and desist when Sandra's voice came out of the handset he was wearing.

"Blake, honey, I think we have a problem," her words were coming out slow, like she was talking with a mouth full of cotton.

"Sandra? Sandra?" Blake almost shouted into the handset.

When he didn't get an answer, he repeated it a few times. Bobby and Melissa walked in, their eyes going wide as they saw the fear and uncertainty in Blake's face.

"What's going on?" Bobby asked.

"Sandra," Blake said, starting to pant.

"Where's Mommy?" Chris asked, coming out from the kitchen with Lisa in tow.

"Mom, can you get Chris here some sort of treat," Blake said, not wanting to break the news.

He didn't know what it was, but it wasn't good.

"Hey Blake," Davis's voice said over the radio, "You missing something?"

Blake turned and if looks could kill, the radio setup would have melted under his fiery gaze.

"What is it Hogg?" Blake spat.

"Your wife, isn't she a lovely thing?" Davis's voice dripped sarcasm.

"Where is she?" Blake said, his voice gone cold.

"Oh, I just took possession. Listen Blake, here's my terms… You turn yourself in for arrest, my men will come and help relocate any survivors and

CRIES OF THE WORLD

divide up food and materials as we see fit. Oh, and all military personnel active or retired are going to report for duty - as they should have already."

"You son of a bitch, what if I don't?" Blake said.

"Well, this is America. I imagine your wife will be charged with war crimes and dereliction of duty. Probably firing squad if I had to guess," Davis said, his voice amused.

"Blake," David whispered, "I have something on their tactical net. They're calling for a helicopter. Sounds like a small team, maybe two or three guys."

Blake took that in and looked around the room. Duncan was still off, but probably listening in, Sgt. Smith was with his men, probably taking down the equipment and getting it ready to transport back up to the Homestead and there was no one else. Blake couldn't ask Lisa, Patty or David to do go with him, and his gaze settled on Bobby. Would Lisa forgive him if he asked her only living son to help?

"I have an idea," Blake told the silent room, "But I may need help. Bobby, Lisa, I really hate to ask but—"

Bobby turned and kissed Melissa deeply before going to the gun rack and pulling Blake's .270 off the shelf. He'd been using Blake's gun more than his own lately and loved how flat shooting and accurate the gun was.

"You two do what you need to. Bring my daughter in law and baby back safely," Lisa said, her eyes watering.

"Where's Mommy? Why is everyone so sad?"

Chris asked.

"Come on, little man, let's go make some fudge or brownies," Lisa told him, leading him towards the kitchen.

"You ready?" Bobby asked.

"Yeah. David, pipe any info to our private tactical channel. Tell Duncan not to worry. Tell him to keep the line clear if possible. I'm going to be moving fast and…"

"Go," Patty said softly, "you can do this."

Blake grabbed his bolt action .30/06 and a box of shells. He put half of each of them in his pockets after filling the gun and paused to consider before grabbing a Glock from their ever growing collection and clipping a holster on. Bobby nodded and they took off at a run, leaving a shocked silence behind them.

Bobby had thought he was in shape before he moved to the Homestead, but living on the hills and working constantly had toughened him up to a level he'd never imagined before. His muscles had muscles and the definition he'd tried hard for in the gym was finally there. As he tried to keep up with Blake, he had to marvel at the strength and endurance of the older man. He had a bum leg and his shoulder had had a big hole in it not months ago, but he ran like the devils of hell were chasing him.

Blake slowed down and paused at a depression in the grass and looked around a bit and then took off running again, not saying a word but pulling his rifle to bear. Bobby only got two big lungful's of air before they were running hard again and he fell to the wayside a bit. Blake finally slowed down and stopped when he got to the edge of the woods to put his handset radio by his ear.

"This is Blake," he said softly.

"Blake, this is Duncan," Duncan's voice came out of the static of the radio, and Blake walked quietly as he listened, "They were talking about an LZ near a clearing. They gave coordinates, but I don't have any maps handy here that would…"

"I know, but I think I know where they are going." Blake said softly.

"Where?"

"The Slaver's camp. I'm following the trail now," Blake said into the handset.

"That's what we're thinking. You can't follow them though, it's a trap, it has to be."

"I know," Blake said.

"Dammit, Blake, you're going to get yourself killed. Stop and give us some time to come help."

"There's no time," Blake said pausing to look at the ground, "do what you can and so will I. Blake out." He said, turning off the radio as Duncan tried pleading again.

Bobby was catching his breath and he wiped the sweat off his brow and looked up at his brother in law. "What's the plan?" he panted.

"They die, we don't," Blake said simply.

Blake and Sandra were somewhat legendary for their well thought out plans and ideas. This simple one didn't sit well with Bobby, but he'd follow Blake through hell and back. Even when his brother died, Blake had done all he could. Now all he had was his mom, Melissa and Blake. He used to have a crush on Sandra, but she'd been Blake's woman through and through.

"Ok, let me know what you need me to do when the time comes," was all Bobby said in reply.

They picked up their pace considerably, almost a jog. Blake only slowed when he was checking the trail for fresh marks. To him it looked like they gave up on dragging Sandra, and somebody had carried her. It made tracking only marginally harder, but he couldn't sprint and follow it. A short time later, he heard the sound of motors and slowed as the clearing the Slavers had set up camp in came into view through the openings in the trees. At the far end, a red smoke streamer had been lit, the smoke blowing away from Blake and Bobby.

"I can't see them," Blake said, bringing his scope up to bear.

"I'll look too," Bobby said, moving behind a tree and glassing the area.

"Duncan said this was a trap; do you think they expected us to follow them out the same trail?" Blake said, starting to worry.

"Maybe. Unless they are right behind us—" Bobby's words cut off as a cold object was pressed into his ear.

"Uh, Blake…"

Blake stood and three men, including the one

with the gun to Bobby's head, melted out of the shadows, one of them carrying Sandra's limp form over his shoulder.

"Looks like we have more folks for Mr. Davis to interrogate," the leader of the three man team said, chewing on a match stick, an ugly smile on his face.

Murderous, cold, deadly.

"When the chopper lands, you three are all going to get on it with us. Throw your guns down and if there's any funny shit, I'm going to open the woman up first before lighting you both up. Which one of you is Blake?"

Bobby didn't mean to, but he looked over to try to see how Blake was doing. His look gave everything away.

"Ok, so you're Blake," the soldier said, "I've heard a lot about you, but I always heard you and your wife were a lot smarter than this. It was almost too easy. I'm really disappointed to find out you're nothing more than a dumb hillbilly."

"You wouldn't be saying that if it were just you and me," Blake said, standing to his full height.

"Yeah, like I'm going to do that. I know who your wife is; she's famous in Black Op's circles. She did some shit so secret that she can't even tell her own father about it. I doubt you know any of that, but I'm sure some of her training has rubbed off on you, from what I've heard. I'm not stupid and I've already got a gun to your head. Now sit, and be silent for a couple minutes."

That chilled Blake. He'd heard things about

his wife from people claiming to know about her, and he knew she wasn't a simple door gunner and mechanic. She might have been when she had first joined up, but her hand to hand and firearm skills were top notch. She'd also whipped up some battle plans on the fly that Duncan could only help to improve slightly. That took training and experience. Blake marveled at what his wife had done in service of the country, and what the man really knew about her.

The uniform read 'Wilson', and he could make out 'Stevens' on the other. The man holding Sandra had his nametag obscured. It was weird and stupid and humiliating all at once. He'd let Wilson's men take him without a shot, without a fight. He'd let his worry, anger and fear overtake his reasoning and now they were caught. Probably dead soon.

The sound of rotors filled the air with a 'whump whump whump' sound, as an old Vietnam era Huey started flaring and floating down towards the opening in the trees. It was still fifty feet off the ground when Blake felt the gun pressed into the back of his neck.

"Who am I kidding? They're going to execute us and leave us here," Blake thought to himself, already sickened by his own resignation.

The gun dug in harder to the back of his head and two gunshots rang out. Blake looked to the left to see Bobby. The man who'd held Bobby at gunpoint was slowly falling to the ground and Blake chanced a look over his shoulder. Wilson was turning, his

CRIES OF THE WORLD

.45 no longer pointed at Blake's head.

Melissa was ten yards behind them, a .45 already coming up to fire. Her bullets hit Wilson in the stomach and chest, and the last one exited the back of his head, painting the forest edge with gore. Blake was already moving, rolling towards his rifle. The man holding Sandra put his own handgun to Sandra's prone form and everyone froze.

"Melissa," Blake said, putting the man's head right in the sights of his deer gun, "don't. If he shoots Sandra, he won't get out of here alive." Blake said.

In truth, he knew Melissa was a good shot, but he didn't want to risk her and the baby on two months of training and practice. He knew he was good enough, but even a shot to the head could let the nerves twitch enough to pull the trigger. He needed an opening…

"See, I'm going to walk out and get on the chopper and you guys aren't going to do anything about it…" The soldier was saying, "and nobody has to die. You got it?"

A deep roaring, then a buzzing like a possessed chainsaw, ripped the soundwaves to shreds as an APC crested the hill, white tracer rounds walking the fire right into the side of the chopper. The explosion was huge and Blake looked back to look at the man holding Sandra for half a heartbeat. The soldier had dropped his gun hand to his waist in shock and was starting to recover from his surprise when Blake put a bullet right into his forehead.

BOYD CRAVEN

Melissa ran as the soldier slumped and caught Sandra's fall even before Blake could get his feet under him.

"Oh my god, oh my god…" Blake kept saying over and over checking her pulse.

It was strong, but she must have been drugged. He pulled his wife close to him and held her, waiting on the APC. He had a good idea who was driving, but he gave his handset to Bobby to ask for help as he put his hand to Sandra's stomach, praying that whatever they drugged her with wouldn't hurt the baby. He knew Duncan was going to be angry, but he could live with that along as his wife was ok.

CHAPTER 9

MICHAEL & KING

The plan they came up with was simple. They'd wait until full dark to go in. With most of the guards at the gate, they were planning on pulling in with the APC, a known unit. They'd park it in the motor pool, get Michael's mother and Chad's lady friend he'd met there, and make their escape. Chad had fallen head over heels in love with a redheaded woman he called Rose. She was barely 5' tall according to what he was saying and he claimed he had no problem fading with them back into the woodwork. Through long conversations, Michael had slowly come to trust Chad, whose real name was almost unpronounceable.

That was also in line with everything that King had seen and heard at the old camp. The defectors who didn't defend the camp gave up, to be released. Those who'd abused the women had been executed by their victims. Word had spread about the camps getting released, and quite often guards would disappear into the night time, never to return to duty. The NATO men were told that what they were doing was necessary work, or the whole country would fail. The problem was, NATO was ran by a coalition or a committee of sorts. Things were misinterpreted or ignored and orders were slipshod and little made sense.

The men they'd stolen the APC from had repeatedly called for Chad, and then radioed the base. Apparently the faults of their particular APC were known by all, and more than once they had indicated that the radio also was an issue. Chad wasn't where he was supposed to be when the team walked half the night… So they figured he'd gotten lost or told them the wrong direction. For once, Murphy was working with the Americans as they drove up slowly, full of fear and confidence.

Michael grinned as he listened to Chad talk to King. A day ago he'd been almost too scared to even look at the giant of a man, but they were talking as if they had known each other for years. Hopes, dreams… a life to look forward to once the disaster righted itself, if it ever did in this lifetime. Michael let his thoughts wonder to his last conversation with his dad before their cruise… How he'd been grounded. How much things had changed, how Michael had grown as both a man and human. He hoped his mother was alive and well, and that she could accept the new 'him'.

The APC drove right down the street and stopped at the fence, gating off the compound.

"Here goes nothing," King said quietly as another guard came out, mirror on a telescopic stick.

He checked the under carriage of the APC and then motioned to another, who unlocked and rolled the gate back. Either these guys hadn't gotten the radioed info, or they weren't paying attention to the APC's numbers as it rolled through and past them. The gate guard gave them half a wave and then pulled the gate closed behind them.

"How many APCs are based here?" King asked.

"Two, this transport and then the … Gunner?" Chad asked, struggling for the words.

King nodded, "That's like a howitzer on it, kid," and they drove back to a large open sided sheet metal building and parked in the darkness near another APC.

Michael put his rifle to the rifle port as Chad crawled out first. He walked over to the other APC and climbed up to look in the hatch. King exited and slowly walked over to it, feeling the engine compartment to the heavily armed brother of their machine.

"Cold," King said simply.

Michael didn't quite trust Chad completely, but King did, from what he could tell. Michael left his pack, but made sure he had extra magazines for his rifle in his vest and that both .45s were topped off, with spare magazines. If it all went well, they would make their escape without gunfire. If Murphy of Murphy's Law poked his nose in, well… Michael wanted to be prepared.

"This way," Chad said after climbing out of the hatch and joining the two men on the ground.

"Follow, don't try to march," Chad said softly as they followed him, "We are units from all over world. Just be casual. No nerves here."

"Now he tells me," King griped softly and Michael had to grin.

The big guy's sense of humor was starting to emerge. They had no issues as they walked across the compound; they even had a guard wave to them in the gloom as they passed him. Michael marveled at that but part of it made a twisted sort of sense… So many guys thrown together to do a job and with so many coming and going, the uniform was the only thing they looked at. Even King's enormous size didn't make the second guard look more than once.

"Do you know where the women are?" King said once they went into what looked like a decommissioned school, the hallways silent.

"Yes, I'm not always a driver. I'm usually a guard here, but the normal driver drank some unfiltered water and…"

"Murphy has been working for us all along," King marveled.

"Yeah, he has. I can't believe our good luck."

CRIES OF THE WORLD

Michael said.

"Damn son, now you done jinxed us," King remarked sorrowfully.

They passed door after door until Chad stopped at one. He pulled out a keychain with well-worn keys.

"Is it time for the bathroom already?" a voice called out of the darkened room.

"No, I need Rose. She awake?" Chad said.

"I know why you need Rose," a feminine voice chuckled and the room filled with giggles as the women teased each other and, apparently, Rose too.

A small form walked out of the darkness and into the barely lit hallway, her hands covering her eyes as she let her eyes adjust to the emergency lights.

"Chad?" She asked, looking at Michael and King.

"Hold," Chad said, closing and locking the door behind her as some good natured catcalls called out.

Rose didn't hold still for long, she leapt into Chad's arms, burying her head in his neck and hugged him fiercely.

"Wow, I didn't know women could be so dirty mouthed…" Michael said, going pink at some of the suggestions that were coming from the darkened room.

"Rose, now is the time. These are friends and they will help. Do you remember where… Michael, what is your mother's name?"

"Last name is Lewiston," Michael said by rote.

"Yeah, she's with laundry, down the hall. Should be done by now, but who knows?"

Chad swore under his breath and King gave Michael an uneasy glance and followed him.

"What's laundry?" Michael asked Rose, a pretty woman a few years older than him, her hair cut short.

"The unit who does the bases laundry. They all work shifts. 24/7. I don't remember what shift Mrs. Lewiston is, I just remember her because I was in there getting my stuff when they pulled her out for questioning two or three weeks ago," Rose whispered back.

Michael knew why she'd been questioned. He was the reason... His father was a trouble maker and Lukashenko had probably radioed ahead for a pickup or Evac somehow. Of course he remembered sending the wife of a dissident to another camp, and had probably told them to grill her. He only hoped she was fine.

"Should we check the dorm first?" Chad asked, indecision gnawing at his features.

"Sure. No guards in the dorm?" King asked.

"No, not this time of night. Everyone is locked in, and guards are in laundry. We don't have a working camera operation yet so it's limited..."

"Everything's limited," Michael muttered.

Chad jingled the keys till he found the right one.

"Mrs. Lewiston?" Chad called.

"Whoizzit?" a sleepy voice called.

"Mrs. Lewiston in here, or is she working?" Chad asked as several forms moved in the darkness.

The creaking of the cots or bunks could be heard in the near silent hallway now.

"She's got the 11-7am shift," a woman said, coming into the light.

Her eyes grew wide as she saw Rose standing with King and Michael behind the guard.

"Is something wrong?" The woman asked suspiciously.

"No, thank you for your cooperation," Chad said starting to swing the door closed.

An arm stopped it, probably painfully.

"What's going on?" the woman asked.

Michael had a sinking feeling and, for once, he couldn't argue with Murphy. He didn't feel right about just getting his Mom out and leaving everyone else.

"Nothing, please step back, I'll be along shortly to explain."

"No, I have a right to know, I…."

Chad pulled the door open, almost pulling the woman off her feet.

"I'm sorry, I have no time for this," he said and pushed her.

The woman's butt hit the floor at the same moment Chad was closing and locking the door.

"We can't leave them all behind," Michael told King.

The big man gave Michael a soulful look and

nodded. "Let's get your momma first," his deep voice bounced off the cement walls.

§ § §

The laundry was at the far end of the hallway. King followed a couple seconds after Chad, who'd struck up a quick conversation with someone. Michael came around the corner in time to see King deliver one big meaty blow to the side of another guard's head. He slumped and Michael brought his rifle up and stopped the guard on the far side of the room's movement towards his sidearm.

"Sergei, no!" Chad said, "This is it, the time we were talking about."

"It is?" The guard said, his face starting to smile.

"Yes, but I must have the Lewiston woman. Her son is here."

"My son?" Michael's mother said into the suddenly silent room that had, seconds before, been noisy with the murmur of female voices.

"Mom?" Michael asked and King gently pulled the rifle from his hands before his Mother almost tackled him to the ground in a fierce hug.

"Oh my God, you've grown so big, and your hair! You aren't eating right, you've gotten so skinny, my God I missed you. Your father is going to be ecstatic, I can't wait—"

"I love you too Mom," Michael said, his words half drowned out as he fought to hug her back and not get suffocated at the same time.

CRIES OF THE WORLD

Michael was a big guy, nowhere near King's size, but his Mom was taller still than Michael and his father.

"Where's your Dad? Did you… Wait, who are…" the realization crept into her eyes and she looked at King and then her son in shock.

"That other camp, that was you?" she asked quietly.

"Mostly friends, but yeah…"

"And your father?" she asked, squeezing the life out of him.

"He's…. Mom… Lukashenko…"

"No…." she pulled away from Michael and looked into his eyes.

He never had been a good liar, and she saw the truth he couldn't say out loud. She bit her lip and looked at King.

"You here to break us all out too?" she asked.

King took her hand in both of his and looked down into her eyes.

"I promise to do the best I can, ma'am," he said humbly.

"What's the plan?" Sergei asked as the women started to chat excitedly, their voices raised.

"Shut it," Chad shouted to them and when the room fell silent, "You," he pointed to a woman and tossed her the keys, "unlock all the doors to the rooms. Tell everyone not to move until we make some noise. You'll know it when we bust through the gate. We'll be the diversion and you melt into the night.

"But my kids, my husband," another woman asked.

"We can do this much for sure," Chad said, "The silver-looking keys are for the men's dorms. Take your kids with you. Keys there as well."

"Oh, God, we're really doing this?" Sergei asked them and everyone but Mrs. Lewiston nodded.

"How are we busting through the gate?" Michael's mother asked.

"Tank. Drive forward, backwards. Drive over the fence. Make a lot of noise. Maybe shoot some guards," King was blunt and to the point.

"And him?" Sergei asked, nodding to the unconscious man.

"I don't care, he cheated at poker," Chad said, and for some reason was confused when everyone laughed.

§ § §

Sergei, Chad, King, Rose, Michael and his mother Amanda moved quickly in the darkness as the women's dorms became noisy behind them. It was impossible not to make some noise and, even if the guards went in there to lock them all down again, they would soon be distracted by what they were planning on doing.

"Disable the gunner?" Chad asked as everyone was climbing into the APC.

"Wait, I have an idea," Michael said, and they waited for everyone to get in so he could climb back out the ladder.

"What are you doing?" his mother yelled.

"I'm going to drive that one. Chad, you get the front gate, ok?"

"Yeah!" Chad called back.

"Ok, I'm going to hit the fence in a bunch of spots. Just make sure you take out anyone who's shooting. I can't drive and do that. It'll give people more directions to get away."

"You won't be able to use the guns, I do not even know how to do this!" Chad called back.

"I'm going to use it as a battering ram. Just don't leave me behind when I'm done!" Michael called, closing the hatch and locking it.

The radio crackled and Michael sat down in the driver's seat and reached for it.

"Kid, you don't got to do this," King said.

"Yeah man, I do. I watched Chad enough to know how to drive this," he said, firing up the dual diesels.

"This isn't just a hit and run escape no more, what you're planning on doing…"

"You said these things were like a tank. I'm just going to wreck the fences and bug out, ok?"

"Michael," his mother's voice on the radio said, "Please turn it off and come back."

"Sorry Mom, Chad's driving that one and, unless Sergei is a driver, I think I'm the only other qualified person."

There was a silence and then the second APC fired up. Michael let out a whoop and gave the twin diesels some pedal. The APC almost leapt out of the enclosure. Michael clipped a support beam coming out, not realizing how hard the steering was.

"Ooops," he said into the radio and then laughed as Michael's mother commented, "You drive like my grandma."

The engine roared as he took off in the opposite direction to the gate. Chad had told him that the supply depot was back there. He didn't want to ruin it, but it backed up to a swampy area, making it easy for people to melt away into the bayou. He didn't plan on going far off the grass, not knowing whether APCs got stuck easy, but it wasn't worth finding out.

"Time to shake things up," Michael said as he rammed the fence, sending chain link and razor wire scattering as the machine tore through it like a hot knife through butter.

§ § §

"He is the best one for what he is proposing," Chad said, sitting in the driver's seat and firing up his own ride.

They watched as the APC leapt forward and clipped one of the poles that supported the structure. The wooden beam crunched and the roof sagged in that direction.

"Ooops," Michael said in the radio.

"You drive like my grandmother," Michael's mom was saying, laughing from happiness and nerves and choking down feelings of pride for her son.

"He's going to be OK in there?" she asked King.

"The thing's a tank. Nothing but a rocket would have a chance to... Oh, Momma, check the boy out!" King pointed, even though he was looking through a slit where the shooting port was.

Chad gave the APC some gas and it roared forward before the roof collapsed on top of them. It came down in a crash that was barely audible over the roar of the twin diesels. Driving down to the base, they had taken it easy, but for the breakout they were using full power and accelerating quickly to the top speed of almost 55 miles per hour. It wasn't hard enough of an acceleration to throw a person back in their seat, but the torque involved in getting such a heavy war machine moving made as much noise as it did when the panicked guards fired on the APC as it refused to slow, and barreled towards the gate.

King stuck the rifle out of the port and fired. He missed, but the dirt erupted and the guards quit firing, jumping out of the way as the heavy vehicle tore the gate off its hinges.

"That was easy," Chad said, coming to a stop a hundred yards beyond the gate.

"Too easy." Amanda said.

"Michael, do you think?" Chad asked.

They winced as more bullets dinged off the armored sides and King pushed the port closed so a lucky shot didn't ricochet inside.

"I feel bad about leaving everyone as well. Rear monitor shows the women starting to flee. The guards are trying to round them... Oh, Gods!" Chad saw chaos erupting.

King strode forward and looked at the small monitor. Michael's APC was crashing through a guard tower, only to reverse and let it fall as he backed into another one. Somewhere, flames were taking hold and the destruction and chaos caused by the women had the handful of people on duty scrambling to try to regain control.

"Want to go back and run over some things?" King asked Michael's mother.

She nodded.

King opened the gun port on the other side as something flashed past the APC and an explosion rocked the night, ringing their heads.

"RPGs!" Sergei screamed.

Chad pointed the APC towards the camp and took in the sight.

Four men had all lined up at the gate. Three of them had RPGs held high, and the fourth was reloading.

"Will that kill us?" Sergei asked.

"No, armor up front is thick. Takes something bigger to do that, unless all of them hit us in same spot. I think. Shit, I'm not a driver normally," Chad complained as Rose rubbed his shoulder.

"What's the kid up to?" King asked.

"Oh Michael," his mother moaned.

CRIES OF THE WORLD

§ § §

Michael was lining up to follow the other APC when he saw a stream and explosion in front of him. He lined his APC up square on the gate and gulped. Four men were standing there, each of them armed with what looked like a bazooka or an RPG. One of them was lining up to fire on Michael, who slid out of the chair and dropped to the floor as the rocket hit the front of the APC. The armor absorbed the explosion, but the concussion of the blast was enough to make his ears ring and his head hurt.

"Shoot at me?" Michael said, but he couldn't hear anything.

He'd never fired anything as big as the gun on the APC, but he'd watched war movies. He'd even seen a John Wayne or Elvis movie where they were in the Navy. The ship had fired off huge bullets that took quite a few men to load. It was nowhere near that big but it looked like what he'd seen in that movie. He looked around and saw the rounds on the shelves to the side and smiled. Big gun or little gun? Being 17, and fascinated with things that went boom, he worked the lever on the breach of the main gun and opened it. A shell fell out and he pushed it back in, locking the breach.

"Already loaded," he mumbled to himself, though he couldn't hear.

Another rocket impacted against the front. He heard that one, and it knocked him off his feet.

"Handles, check." He turned some switches on until the handles turned the turret...

"Up and down," Michael murmured, noticing how hot it was getting inside, and wiping sweat away.

The sweat trickled down his arm and he saw it was a red smear. He wiped at his ears and shrugged. Not much he could do about it.

"Now, how do I fire this thing? Where's the trigger?" Michael said, aiming about ten feet in front of the soldiers, trusting the blast to take them out.

He found a button with 'огонь' printed on it. It was the only red button and red buttons usually meant...

"Fire," he hollered, rocking backwards as the main gun went off.

Through the viewfinder he saw that the men didn't blow up in a fiery explosion, they exploded in a red gore.

Michael went and sat back down in the driver's seat, trying to listen to roar of the motor to see if it had been damaged, but he couldn't hear anything. Wiping his ear out with his sleeve he put the monster vehicle in gear and drove forward.

"That wasn't so hard, now was it?" Michael said, his head hurting horribly now.

Nobody in the APC next to him got out so Michael looked and waited. Soon a flood of bodies started fleeing and he could see from them surging past his unit on the monitors. People banged on it in thanks, but he couldn't hear them. He realized the reason for the blood and the reason everything was so quiet.

"This is Michael," he said into the radio, not able to hear himself, "I'm ok. I got my bell rung there. I'll follow you guys when you're ready, or pop the hatch when it's safe. The last rocket... I can't hear anything right now." He put the mic down and waited.

The hatch of the APC next to him popped open and he went and unlocked and popped his as well.

His mother was the first one out, and she jumped from one to the other, almost pulling her son off his feet as he tried to get out. He could feel her running her hands through his hair as she pulled his head tightly against her and then felt her pause. Michael looked up to see his Mom talking but he wasn't getting any of it.

"Can't year you. Love you, Mom," he said.

She pulled him and he was climbing down the hatch when his foot slipped. Big strong arms caught him and lowered him to the floor gently. Nice soft floor, he thought, one that would be perfect for sleeping on. Michael laid down a moment, to shut his eyes and was out cold.

§ § §

"Is he ok?" His mother asked king.

"Bell got rung. Concussion, probably burst eardrums." King told her.

BOYD CRAVEN

"That means he is ok, yes?" Sergei asked, losing some of his language as he dogged the hatch down firmly and held on as Rose helped navigate for Chad.

"Yes, he is ok," King told Michael's mother, pulling her son into a sitting position, letting his head rest against his legs.

"You don't talk much, do you?" she asked the gentle giant next to her.

"Nope," King said, ignoring the sharp glace he got.

§ § §

"Where are we now?" Michael asked, sore and uptight from being on the road for close to two weeks.

His hearing had started to come back and he was turning into a nonstop chatter box, showing his mother how much of the boy was still left in her young man.

"Almost to Kentucky, boy." King said.

"Cool. What's in Kentucky?" he asked them.

They'd stopped and were resting on the side of the road while Sergei went to drain fuel from a tanker truck that had stalled.

"People." King said.

"What kind of people?" Michael asked impatiently.

"Good ones."

"Say, Michael," Chad asked, "How did you

know to use the AP round at the gate guys? I've been dying to ask you but we've been driving and you've been deaf..."

"What's an AP round?" Michael asked.

His eyes got wide when all the color drained out of King and Chad's faces.

"What?" Michael asked.

"Anything else would have blown us all up," King said, his voice slow and gravelly as if two boulders were rubbing together... Angry boulders...

"Well, glad that worked out then. I feel bad we couldn't take the other APC but..."

"One more hit from that rocket and you would have been dead," King told him, "The armor couldn't take no more. You got something kid, I don't know if its luck, or balls the size of... Excuse me ma'am," King said when he noticed Michael's mother's disapproving stare.

"You got something kid. Something. We had more luck than anybody should have a right to have. Lukashenko, Chad here, a plan that didn't backfire. You figuring out how to operate the gun and having the right shell. That's some big luck there boy, big luck." King said, one of the longest strings of words anybody had heard from him in a while.

"Or it was his faith, and God's hand guiding him," Michael's mother's voice was calm and soothing.

"So you can hear good enough now? Not just couple words here and there?" King asked.

Michael's hearing had been returning in

snatches until he could make out the steady thrum of the diesels as they were moving. Sometimes bits of conversation. He'd gotten an ear infection, but the first aid kit in the APC had syringes with a generic penicillin and morphine. They'd shot him up full of penicillin when his ears started to hurt, discharging fluid, and he slept for a couple days. That healing did the trick and the infection began to dry up. It would be the first day out of the APC without the motors running. He could hear them, but not as loudly as he'd hoped.

"Without the motors running, guys sound faint, but yeah, I can hear you all," Michael said.

"Good, no permanent damage." King said.

"So what's in Kentucky again?" Michael repeated the question, knowing there were some people there John had worked with to help bust him out of the FEMA camp.

"Here boy, want you to listen to this now that we're stopped," King said, handing him the handset.

"What is it?"

"Rebel Radio. Dudes from all over the country are going to the heartland. Organizing. Getting ready."

"Ready for what?" Michael asked, a little breathless, realizing it was the same people John had talked to.

"Some real badasses who fought against all odds," King told him.

"To protect our borders," his mom said, hugging him, "They're coming in through Mexico right now."

"Who is?" Michael asked, hating that he was two weeks behind in information. If he'd only thought to grab a notebook and pen at some of their stops, maybe he'd know and wouldn't be so bored all the time.

"The people who did this to us," King said pointing to the sky.

"The terrorists," Rose said, hugging Chad close.

"What are we going to do in Kentucky?" Michael asked, confused.

"Get organized," King said.

"Then what?" Rose asked.

"We take the fight to them," Michael's mother said, closing the subject, "and we fight to win."

CHAPTER 10

THE HOMESTEAD, KENTUCKY

Sandra awoke to a ton of curious faces surrounding the front porch. She felt strong arms holding her and a gentle swinging motion. Blake held her across his lap, cradling her head and body on the swing.

"Hey," Sandra said, her voice dry and coming out in a croak.

"Hey, yourself. How you feeling?" Blake said.

The silence was eerie; there must have been twenty people standing around or sitting on the railings, but everyone was so silent, it seemed like they were holding their breath.

"Sore. Stomach and head hurt some," she admitted.

Blake handed her a cup of water. It was still cold from the well, and she had to force herself not to gulp it down.

"They got you with a tranquillizer dart of some kind," Blake told her, pointing to the small blood stain on her shirt.

"Yeah, fast acting. Never saw them," she said between sips.

"Do you think the drugs will hurt the baby?" Blake asked.

"I don't think so," Sandra said, "at least, I hope not. I can still feel him moving around in there," she said, a tired, lazy smile on her face as she put her hands on her stomach.

"Hey," she said after a moment and looking around, "where's Chris?"

"Took a nap, he should be up any time now,"

"How late is it?" Sandra asked, noting that it was either dusk or dawn.

"Almost dark," Blake said, running his hands through her hair.

"Hey, Blake, is my daughter awake?" Duncan's voice came out of the handset on the small table that Blake had fashioned out of old pallets, startling everyone.

"Yes sir," Blake said, grabbing it and handing it to Sandra.

"Daddy?" Sandra asked.

"Yes baby, how you doing?" Duncan said, his voice sounding happy now.

"Good. Daddy, we have to stop Davis. The man must be insane to keep trying this."

"Didn't Blake tell you where Sgt. Smith and I

are at with some of the men?" Duncan said with a chuckle.

"No… I just woke up."

Sandra looked up at Blake who suddenly seemed interested in the sky, the ceiling, or the roof or anything else he could look at but her.

"We uh… Well… I'm in Greenville and we broadcast on all frequencies that we're coming for Davis. Anyone who stands with the lunatic is going to… Well, you know."

"What did they say?" Sandra asked, her voice dry and crackling.

"Davis himself came on, cussing and screaming. Almost sounds like the rats are deserting the ship. Probably doing the right thing finally. Even merc's don't like dying for no reason. Many of them asked for an hour to flee the area."

"Blake, how much artillery did they take?" Sandra asked.

"All of it," Blake said softly, "As well as the APC/MRAPs. They got them tipped over with the help of the old transport truck we stashed."

"Daddy?"

"Yes, dear?"

"Call in the fire, don't get too close."

"None of us are, hon. I'll be on the air with you soon. I'll let you know when it's done. Duncan, out," he said before changing frequencies.

Blake could hear the base set in the house get turned up.

"Hey, kid with the music, you got some Rage

CRIES OF THE WORLD

Against the Machine handy?" Duncan asked the airwaves of Rebel Radio.

"Always man, always," a teenaged voice replied immediately.

"How about Bulls on Parade?" Duncan said, "Lisa suggested it for this and we're going to be playing it on the loud speakers on the APC's. Part of my daughter's psy-ops thing."

"You ready?" the kid asked.

"Yes, son." Duncan said.

The music drifted out of the radio, covering up the muted sounds of a berserker chainsaw on PCP, as Blake listened to the tactical net at the same time the house was playing the Rebel Radio feed. Corinne was calling in the shots and Duncan was barking orders to reload, cover fire. It was chaotic, and it sounded like a video game, but it was real life. Men screamed, muted shouts were heard over the tactical net. Soon a new song came on. Blake recognized it from the few times he'd dialed to the rock station by mistake. The unmistaken sound of "Freedom" started blasting.

The feedback was tremendous and the radio crackled as the signal distorted from the nearness to the loud speakers. When the song was done, the heavy machine guns pounded out their thunderous songs of death for another few moments and then fell silent as the final verse was sung. Blake and Sandra had heard it before, but never before had it felt so poignant to hear the meaning happen in real life.

"Mop up, sir?" Corrine's voice asked.

"No, that was an old school building. Nothing inside could have survived that. Let's pick up and go home," Duncan radioed back.

"Is it over?" Sandra asked into the handset.

"Yes baby, it's over." Duncan said.

§ § §

The night that Sandra had been drugged and Blake and Bobby had taken off at a dead run, Melissa had hesitated. She was a reserve squad member, trained with the others, but because of her only being 18, she was left to the less dangerous roles. She'd gone to the pile of guns and, despite everyone's objections, she took off. She'd gone without Intel or a handset to listen to developments, but the guys' path was easy to follow and, despite things, she'd made it there in time to put two bullets into the man holding Bobby hostage.

The gun barked and bucked just as she thought it would, and she changed targets, making sure that Blake was clear when she fired on him. He dropped, never even suspecting there was someone behind him until the man to his left fell.

Her vision narrowed on the last man holding Sandra and she'd hesitated. It was a tight shot, and she wasn't confident. Then came the helicopter, the explosion and the crash. She let her body fall forwards as Blake took the shot. The man holding Sandra had started to slump in slow motion, and

CRIES OF THE WORLD

she was able to roll close and take Sandra's weight as the man collapsed.

Sandra's hot breath and warm body told her she was still alive, but it had been a close thing. After the APC arrived and Duncan loaded them all up, it took them back, clearing a path through the forest as the armored vehicle literally pushed small trees and obstacles out of the way. Duncan was more than a little disturbed and ranting in a way Melissa had never seen from a preacher, but she understood the anger. His sons in law, his only daughter, his grandchild…

She'd gotten back to find her Father and Mother standing there, their faces full of shock, hurt.

"Why'd you run out on us like that?" Curt, her father, demanded.

"They had Bobby," she'd told him shortly.

"You're not some soldier, you're just…" Curt began.

"She is a soldier," Curt's wife spoke up, pushing out of his arms, "For months now, she's trained, she's fought, she's learned. Don't you try to take her hard work away from her!"

"But she could have been killed, or hurt! Over some boy who keeps—"

"Daddy, I love him," Melissa said, stepping into Bobby's arms.

"And I love her too. I was going to ask your permission to marry her, now that she's old enough, but maybe you and I won't ever see eye to eye." Bobby said, his voice cold and emotionless.

145

"Excuse me?" Curt blurted, not quite covering up the gasp his wife let slip out.

"If you dislike me so much sir, then I'll marry her without your permission. We're both adults now and you're more than a little bit over-protective," Bobby said, taking Melissa by the hand and starting to leave.

"Wait!" Curt yelled, his face red.

"Yes?" Bobby and Melissa asked.

"Melissa, I'm sorry. Bobby is a nice... Oh shit, fine. Yes, Bobby, you have my permission," Curt thrust out his hand, and, with a grin, Bobby walked up and tried not to wince as Curt crushed his hand in a very firm shake and whispered to him.

"Someday when you are a father," Curt whispered, "and you have a daughter or two, you'll understand why it's so hard to let go. Don't hurt her."

"I won't. Thanks Curt," Bobby said, smiling despite the pain.

§ § §

Weeks had gone by, and the only excitement was Sgt. Silverman sending out three of his best mechanics to the Homestead. Farm equipment isn't a whole lot different than other diesel powered equipment, and, with the tractor dealerships nearby, they were able to cobble enough together to get a couple combines and various tractors started. Crewing them and putting the food up would be for the homestead to decide. Blake's crew would get what they needed, and the newly formed militia guard co-ran by Silverman and Sandra would help distribute it. Things would get back to normal somehow, or they would deal with things as it came.

"Hey, Blake, Chris?" Sandra called softly, knowing it was time for Rebel Radio.

"Yeah?" Blake asked from the other room.

"Come quick," Sandra said, but her voice didn't sound distressed, she had been relaxing in the bedroom.

Blake came in with a handset, but he'd already asked Patty and David to sit in if there was something specific shot his way during the Q&A.

"Hey Mommy, me and grandma were making cookies," Chris said, crawling up on the bed next to Sandra.

His little body molded it to her side and he smiled and rubbed her stomach, something that had almost become iconic. Blake sat down next to her, still concerned. Sandra rarely was sick, but she hadn't wanted to get out of bed that day. She assured them all she was fine, but Blake couldn't imagine what it was that she was calling them in for.

"Right here," she said, taking both of their hands and pushing them against her stomach.

"Tickles!" Chris giggled.

"Oh wow," Blake said, his face lighting up, "Hey there little dude," a grin tugging at his face.

"Or dudette!" Chris said.

They laughed. It could be a girl! They were all

relieved to be able to feel the baby for themselves. The tranquilizer hadn't hurt the baby after all.

"Blake, honey?" Sandra asked, her eyes moist with unshed tears.

"Yeah? He asked, running his free hand through her hair.

"I love you."

"I love you too," Blake smiled and Chris grinned.

They felt the baby play parkour in Sandra's stomach and everything was all right in the world for them in that moment.

—THE END—

ABOUT THE AUTHOR

Boyd Craven III was born and raised in Michigan, an avid outdoorsman who's always loved to read and write from a young age. When he isn't working outside on the farm, or chasing a household of kids, he's sitting in his Lazy Boy, typing away.

http://www.boydcraven.com/
Facebook: https://www.facebook.com/boydcraven3
Email: boyd3@live.com
You can find the rest of Boyd's books on Amazon:
http://www.amazon.com/-/e/B00BANIQLG

33310747R00096

Made in the USA
San Bernardino, CA
29 April 2016